NOV 2 9 2018

NO LON
SEATTL

D0343062

SLEEPING
IN MY JEANS

NOV 2 9 2016

SLEEPING IN MY JEANS

Connie King Leonard

Ooligan Press
Portland, Oregon

© 2018 Connie King Leonard

ISBN13: 978-1-947845-00-8

All rights reserved. No part of this book may be reproduced or transmitted in any form or by any means, electronic or mechanical, including photocopying, recording, or by any information storage and retrieval system, without permission in writing from the publisher.

Ooligan Press
Portland State University
Post Office Box 751, Portland, Oregon 97207
503-725-9748
ooligan@ooliganpress.pdx.edu
www.ooliganpress.pdx.edu

Library of Congress Cataloging-in-Publication Data
Names: Leonard, Connie King, author.
Title: Sleeping in my jeans / Connie King Leonard.
Description: Portland, Oregon: Ooligan Press, Portland State University, [2018] | Summary: Homeless and alone on the streets, sixteen-year-old Mattie Rollins and her six-year-old sister, Meg, race to discover the fate of their missing mother.
Identifiers: LCCN 2018013008 (print) | LCCN 2018019521 (ebook) | ISBN 9781947845015 (Ebook) | ISBN 9781947845008 (pbk.)
Subjects: | CYAC: Sisters—Fiction. | Homelessness—Fiction. | Single-parent families—Fiction. | Missing persons—Fiction. | Racially mixed people—Fiction.
Classification: LCC PZ7.1.L455 (ebook) | LCC PZ7.1.L455 Sle 2018 (print) | DDC [Fic]—dc23
LC record available at https://lccn.loc.gov/2018013008

Cover design by Jenny Kimura
Interior design by Bridget Carrick

References to website URLs were accurate at the time of writing. Neither the author nor Ooligan Press is responsible for URLs that have changed or expired since the manuscript was prepared.

Printed in the United States of America

For resilient kids
and
For Robby
Your spirit inspires me

CHAPTER ONE

AIR RUSHES AT MY FACE. I stretch my legs out and pump higher and higher, letting the wind wash away the stress of school assignments and everyday life. I love to swing. To feel the freedom of almost flying. To gasp at the top of my arc, just before I fall back to the earth. A smile spreads across my face and peace floods my heart.

Meg, my six-year-old sister, swings beside me, squealing with delight. "Mattie! You're so high!"

It's one of those bright, crisp days in mid-November. Clouds drift over the pale blue sky. Leaves flutter from the trees, sprinkling soggy green grass with pretty little dabs of red, yellow, and orange. It's a day to play in the park, act silly, and be a kid again.

I bend my knees and let myself drift back and forth in a giant arc. Fall is my favorite season—a last-minute splash of color before winter brings on the steady gray of Oregon rain.

I breathe in the cool, sweet crispness of the air, pulling it deep into my lungs. My body slows until I drag my feet to a stop. "Time to go, Megsy."

Some teenagers hate babysitting younger brothers and sisters. Not me. I've taken care of Meg since she was born. The two of us are so close it's like Meg and I are one person, just living life at six and sixteen. If anything happened to her, my body would rip in half and all the love in my heart would bleed out, soak into the soil, and be gone forever.

Meg hops off the swing and grabs my hand. "Sundays are the bestest day of the whole week." She swings my hand extra high. "Mommy's home."

I squeeze her hand and swing it back and forth, high and crazy. Meg breaks into a mass of silly giggles. Sundays are my best day too, for that exact same reason. Mom is home.

When I started high school, Mom decided to finish her GED. She passed her tests with high marks, giving her tons of confidence and getting her excited about her education. Mom signed up for a couple of classes at the community college. She still works her regular job at St. Vincent de Paul, or St. Vinnie's as we call it, but she added Saturdays at 7-Eleven to pay the tuition.

Meg and I kick our way through crunchy, dry leaves on the trek to our apartment. The place really belongs to Darren, Mom's boyfriend. We've lived with him for almost two years, which should mean we're one happy little family, but it's not working out that way.

Meg lets go of my hand and races toward a clump of maple trees sporting brightly colored crowns, spreading their arms over our heads like umbrellas. No matter what the season or how crummy the weather, this is always our favorite spot on the way home from school. Meg reaches down, grabs a leaf, and holds it up for me to see. "Look! It's giant!"

I dig through a pile of leaves spilling over the plain gray sidewalk. "They're like fire," I say, "all crackly and warm and bright."

Meg and I gather up an array of the biggest and most colorful we can find, fanning them out in our hands. I hold them across my face, cock my head to the side, and peek over the top. "Princess Megan," I say in a high, squeaky voice, "are you having a very fine day?"

Meg sticks out her hip, rests her hand on it, and fans herself with her leaves. "A very fine day, Queen Mattie. An extra-specially fine day."

We giggle and play pretend while we tromp the rest of the way home. Having a baby sister is the best. I get to color pictures, build sand castles, and go to tea parties. I can play Candy Land and Go Fish all day while Mom works and not worry about homework, money, or a college scholarship. When I'm with Meg, I'm young and happy.

Our neighborhood is in the north part of Eugene and consists of a string of older apartments off a busy street. It's not a place with a cute playground for kids, and it's not surrounded by wide green lawns and attractive landscaping for the grown-ups. The apartment building is a functional, no-frills kind of place, with a roof, doors that lock, and living room windows that overlook the parking lot.

The inside of Darren's apartment is as plain and simple as the outside. White walls. White blinds on the windows. Faded tan carpet in the living room and two small bedrooms. Mom gave Darren's apartment a bit of style. She bought a picture of Paris at a garage sale and hung it over the couch, and she found one of New York City at St. Vinnie's. She put that one right by the door, so we see it every time we leave the apartment. On the little table near the front window, she set a plant with round, glossy green leaves. Framed photos of Meg and me sit next to it.

Mom is in our mini kitchen cooking spaghetti. "Hey." She gives Meg a hug and grins at me. "Have fun in the park?"

Meg looks like Mom with the same pale skin and dark-blue eyes. My dad was part black, so I look like I don't even belong in the same family. Some people are rude and ask Mom if I'm adopted, and when she says no, they want to know what my dad looked like. Those same people never ask about Meg's dad.

Mostly, I envy Mom's and Meg's hair. It's a soft light brown with hints of blond peeking through—plus it's long, straight, and shiny. Hair I would love to have. Mine is a dark mass of curls I can't manage no matter how hard I try.

I grab a spoon and dip it into the tomato sauce. "We *always* have fun at the park, Mom." The sauce is so hot I have to blow on it before I can put it into my mouth. Mom is a great cook. She makes meals out of just about anything. When money is short, she takes us to the food bank and loads up on whatever they're giving away. Sometimes it's food we've never tasted, like turnips or kale. But that doesn't stop her from taking it home, looking up a recipe, and making something out of it. She doesn't waste anything.

Mom snatches the spoon out of my hand and waves us out of the kitchen. "Go. Finish your homework. Darren said he'd be home by six."

Darren's not my dad, and he's not Meg's. Mom dated him for six months before she agreed to move into his apartment. Darren's halfway decent to us when Mom's around, but when she's gone, he ignores us like Meg and I are pieces of furniture. Obstacles in his way. We don't complain, though. Living with him would be worse if he hassled us all the time.

Our bedroom is small, with a low bookcase separating twin beds. A dresser sits near the door, and one small closet holds the rest of our clothes, shoes, toys, and whatever else we need to stash. Sharing space with Meg doesn't bother me. She's like my security blanket, a comfort to have sleeping so close that I can reach out and almost touch her.

Meg goes directly to her favorite toy, which is the dollhouse she got from Santa. Mom found it at St. Vinnie's, cleaned it up, and bought her a couple of inexpensive dolls and some little furniture to go with it. Meg loves it and plays with it for hours at a time.

I flop on my bed and sort through my homework. My goal is a college scholarship. So far, keeping a 4.0 grade average hasn't been a problem, but high school is way harder than middle school—plus the stakes are a whole lot higher. I'm afraid that if I get one little B+, I'll lose my chances at full tuition and end up waiting tables at an all-night truck stop for the rest of my life.

At six, Mom calls us back to the kitchen. Darren expects Mom to have dinner ready when he gets home, even on days when she's working a full shift. He never cleans the apartment, shops for groceries, or does the laundry. Sometimes I get disgusted with Mom for letting Darren use us like we're his own personal maid service. Mom says he pays the rent and utilities, and that's huge. Plus, she says most men she knows don't cook, clean, or help in the house. I say Darren's getting off way too easy.

We putter around, getting dinner ready to eat. Meg gets the garlic bread and sets it on the table while I grab salad dressings from the refrigerator. Mom drains the spaghetti and dumps it in a bowl.

I'm starving, so I plop into my chair and hope Mom lets us start without Darren. Meg does the same. Mom pulls out her phone and fires off a text. We wait.

By now it's almost six thirty. "Can we eat, Mom?" I say. "The spaghetti's getting cold."

Mom repeats herself. "Darren said he'd be home by six."

Darren makes a lot of promises he doesn't keep. Quitting drinking and saving his money to take classes for a contracting license are just the beginning of the list.

"Mommy?" says Meg. "Can we start? Please?"

Mom wants the four of us to live like a sweet little family, even if only for a Sunday night dinner of spaghetti and garlic bread. I get it. Her dad was a drug addict who died of an overdose when he was only twenty-five, and her mom was an alcoholic who neglected her so badly the state took her away when she was eight. After that, she drifted through foster care until she got pregnant with me. Some of her foster homes were decent and treated her well, but others were not. None of them were stable or permanent.

Seconds tick off the kitchen clock before she finally says, "Okay. Let's eat." The disappointment written on Mom's face makes my heart hurt.

Meg and I dive in. Mom spends most of the meal twirling spaghetti around on her plate.

CHAPTER TWO

DARREN BEATS ON THE DOOR and wakes us all up at midnight. "Rita! Open up the damn door."

This isn't the first time I've been woken up in the night. Neighbors come home late or drink too much, forgetting some of us have to go to school or work in the morning. Family problems boil to the surface when the rest of us are tired and want to sleep. Sometimes the red and blue lights of police cars flash through our bedroom window. At least the lights tell me the cops are here, so everything will get sorted out and I can go back to sleep.

He pounds and pounds until Mom gets up and lets him in. The neighbor beside us bangs on the wall next to my bed.

Meg whispers, "Mattie?" Her voice quivers with a near sob. "Is Darren drunk?"

I crawl out of bed and slide in beside her. "Yeah. Sounds like it."

Meg and I snuggle together and listen to the fight. Mom tries to keep her voice down, but Darren doesn't make any attempt to be quiet. This isn't the first fight we've witnessed in person or through our bedroom wall, but that doesn't make it any easier. Meg puts her hands over her ears. I hug her close and wonder why Mom stays with him.

Angry words pound at the walls of our bedroom. Part of me wants to listen to all the ugly details. The other part of me tries to shut out their voices or at least pretend it's the wife beater next door and not my own mother fighting with her boyfriend.

Their voices stop, but the silence is scarier. I hold my breath and listen to the struggle of bodies, the grunts and moans and physical contact. Mom cries out and furniture crashes. Meg and I jerk upright, but Meg doesn't sit frozen in bed like me. She pushes out of my arms and flies for the door. I throw myself out of bed and run after her.

Meg flings open the door to our room and races down the hall. I grab her before she dives into the middle of Mom and Darren's fight. Meg struggles in my arms, but I pull her close.

The apartment is dark except for a night-light in the hallway and a single light bulb over the kitchen stove, but they are enough to see evidence of the fight. One of the kitchen chairs lies broken on the floor. The others are shoved to the side. Mom leans against the kitchen table with Darren hovering over her.

"Don't you get it, Rita?" He sneers in her face. "You just ain't smart enough."

He backs away, giving me a good look at Mom. Her hair is a mass of tangles. Blood trickles from her nose and the corner of her mouth. The side of her face is red and splotchy. My stomach rolls, sending acid shooting up the back of my throat.

Meg screams, "Mommy!"

Every muscle I have quivers, then tightens until my body turns rigid. My face scrunches up so much my teeth hurt from the pressure. I've never seen Mom hurt. Ever. She and Darren have had fights before but never like this. Never this physical.

Darren tips a can of beer to his lips. That's new too. He isn't supposed to bring alcohol into the house. He promised he wouldn't drink at all, but that promise didn't last long. "It's the only way I can hang with my friends," he'd say. "Besides, what's the big deal? It's just one beer." Now, he doesn't even bother to explain why he's drunk and six hours late.

Darren gulps the rest of the beer and squeezes the can until he crushes it in his fist. "You got these high-minded plans, Rita, like you're better than the rest of us. But you just don't get it." He holds the crushed can in front of Mom's face. "College ain't nothin' but a big waste of your money."

Darren throws the empty beer can against the wall. He turns back to Mom and curls his lip. "And you're too dumb to know it." He thrusts the flat of his hand against Mom's chest and pushes her so hard she stumbles backward. The table she's leaning on slides across the floor, knocking over two kitchen chairs.

Meg cries out, wrenching against my arms. Rage sends heat shooting along my nerves, making my muscles twitch with tension. My fingers itch to rip every limb from his body and scratch his face into bloody gashes. The need to hurt Darren is so strong I can hardly hold myself back, but my job

9

is to protect Meg. I hang on tight and turn all my anger into hating him. How dare he tell Mom she's too dumb to go to school when he's the one without a brain or ambition? Darren may pay the rent, but Mom takes care of him like he's the king of a castle instead of a loser going nowhere.

He wheels around. "What're you brats staring at?"

We've shared Mom with Darren for two and a half years, and I resent him for that. I look him right in the eye and say, "You worthless piece of trash."

Darren stalks across the room. He leans toward me until I gag at the smell of beer on his breath. I glare right back at him and refuse to show him one tiny bit of fear. Without a word, he puts his hands on my shoulders and shoves, sending Meg and me stumbling backwards to land against the couch.

Mom leaps at him, screaming, "Don't touch my kids!" Darren waves his arm as if he's swatting away a fly. Mom gropes for a lamp on the end table—searching for anything to throw—but Darren is already out the door.

I let go of Meg. She races across the room, burying her face against Mom's chest. Mom sinks back against the wall and hugs her with one arm, her other hand pressed flat against the side of her face. "Are you hurt, baby?" she whispers. "Are you or Mattie hurt?"

"We're okay, Mom." I step forward, afraid to know how badly Darren beat her. "Are *you* okay?" She turns away, hiding behind her hair.

"Mom?" I step closer, reach over, and pull her hand away. The pale skin around her eyes is already turning purple and puffy. I take a deep breath and try to keep my voice from shaking. "You need ice, Mom."

"Grab garbage bags, Mattie." Her words come out garbled, slurred together from pain and swelling. "Get you and Meg dressed. Pack clothes, but only what you both need." She takes a deep ragged breath. "And all your blankets, baby."

"Mommy," wails Meg. "What's happening?"

Mom gently pushes her away. "Go with Mattie, sweetie. Help her pack."

I race to the kitchen and yank a box of garbage bags out from under the sink, peeling off the last of the roll. I grab a sandwich bag out of the drawer, run over to the freezer, and dump in a bunch of ice. Meg clutches at Mom, but I pull her away and hand Mom the ice. "Come on, Megs."

I steer my sister into our bedroom and help her strip off her pajamas. She puts on underwear, jeans, and a sweater while I get dressed as quick as I can. But then I waste valuable seconds standing in the middle of the room, wondering where to start. Clothes. I throw open a dresser drawer. "Hold the bag, Meg." I sort through Meg's underwear, socks, t-shirts, and jeans, trying to pick out what we'll need. When the bag is full, I tie the top shut and grab another one. Sorting takes too long, so I stuff in anything I can grab, cramming Meg's dresses in with my jeans and sweaters.

Mom comes in and grabs the first two bags. "Hurry, girls. Grab your blankets."

Meg scoops up her stuffed animals and jams them in with her pajamas. I glance around the room, wondering what I've forgotten. Drawers hang half out of the dresser with dribbles of clothes draped over their sides. The closet door stands open. Hangers litter the floor, jumbled together with old toys and beat-up tennis shoes. My books sit in perfect rows on our little bookshelf. Fantasy. Classics. Trashy romances. All mine. All carefully collected. The garbage bags are full, so I can't take them.

Mom sticks her head in the door. "Girls!"

Meg and I throw on our backpacks. I hand Meg the pillows, scoop blankets off our beds, and push Meg toward the door. We hurry out of the apartment, and there's Darren standing on the sidewalk with a can of beer in one hand and a whole six-pack in the other.

He laughs when he sees us. "Where're *you* going?"

Darren's right. Where are we going? It's the middle of the night. The sky is black, the air misty and cold. The other apartments are dark and so quiet they could be empty. Despair hangs over the building like a shroud.

Mom turns away from the man she's shared her life and family with and herds us toward Ruby, our beat-up Subaru station wagon.

Darren reaches out and grabs Mom by the arm, spinning her around. "I *said* where d'ya think you're going?"

Mom jerks her arm away, leans in, and glares. "You knew when I moved in that I don't live with druggies or drunks or abusers." She pulls back. "And I sure don't live with guys who knock my kids around."

Darren throws his beer can against the apartment building. It hits with a splat, sending a spray of beer streaming down the siding. Mom uses the garbage bags in her hands to push Meg and me toward Ruby. I stuff our blankets and bags in the back, wondering where we're going. It's the middle of the night. Can we find a motel? A room? Are places even open this late?

Mom slides behind the wheel. I shove plastic garbage bags out of the way, settle Meg into the back seat, and jump into the front. Mom starts the car and backs out of her parking spot. We drive away from Darren's apartment, away from our life of nearly two years. Where do we go from here?

Mom leans forward, clutches the wheel with both hands, and drives extra slow. If I were behind the wheel, I'd peel out in a squeal of tires and burned rubber. That way, Darren would know I was so glad to be leaving that I couldn't get away fast enough. But maybe Mom's driving slowly because she's got two kids in the car, her hands are shaking, and tears are running down her battered face, clouding her vision.

The streets in our neighborhood are dark and lonely. No one is out walking their dog in the middle of the night. No one is driving to the store for milk. The whole world feels like it's lost or destroyed, with Mom, Meg, and me the only survivors, cocooned in rusty old Suby Ruby.

The windshield wipers flick back and forth, clearing away the mist. Mom drives to Beltline and takes the eastbound on-ramp. A few cars cruise by, their headlights brightening our way. She drives a couple of miles before turning south into a quiet neighborhood with tall trees and wide front lawns. I wonder what she's doing. We don't know anyone who lives here, and there aren't motels where we could get a room for the night. When Mom parks Ruby beside a clump of trees near a small park, I get it. We're sleeping in the car. No bed. No bathroom. Just the three of us camping out on the street, hoping to survive the night.

I lean toward Mom and whisper. "Can't we get a motel?"

Mom shakes her head. "They're too expensive. Plus, we'll only be out here a few hours."

Meg is so tired she doesn't question why we shove garbage bags around and fold the back seat flat to make a bed. Mom and I spread out the blankets without saying a word. She takes Meg over to the bushes to go to the bathroom. I should go too, but I'm not about to bare my butt this close to civilization.

Meg and I crawl into our makeshift bed. Mom covers us with quilts before she slides into the driver's seat and pulls a blanket around her shoulders. I wrap my arms around my baby sister and hold her until her breath settles into a slow, steady rhythm. It's only then that I hear Mom crying into her pillow.

I should comfort her—pat her shoulder and tell her we'll be okay—but all I can do is stare into the dark. How safe is it for girls to sleep in a car, anyway? Mom locked the doors, but women joggers get nabbed even during the day. We're out here in the middle of the night when creeps could be lurking behind the bushes or around a corner, ready to pounce on their next victims.

Fear gnaws at me, eating up my self-control. Do predators sniff out their quarry, like lions stalking the weakest in the herd? Do they know where to look and when their prey is most vulnerable? Even protected by Ruby's sturdy body, sleeping in the car makes us easy pickings for any scumbag that happens along.

Somehow, I fall asleep.

CHAPTER THREE

A GARBAGE TRUCK RUMBLES BY and wakes me to the early gray of morning. I close my eyes, take in a long, deep breath, and blow it out, slow and steady. We survived.

Mom drives us to one of those all-night gas stations near the freeway. The three of us race to the bathroom, past truckers paying for fill-ups and fistfuls of Twinkies. Mom takes Meg in one stall, and I almost jerk the door off another in my hurry to get my jeans down.

We clean up in the grime of the gas station. Yellow lights over the dirty mirror turn my skin a dull, sick shade of brown. I dab at my face with a wet paper towel. Mom says my skin is my best feature, next to my brown eyes. I try to believe her, but I've spent my life as one of the only black kids in school, so I can't help feeling different.

My hair sticks out in a halo of dark frizz, and I realize my hairbrush is back at Darren's apartment. Mom has a comb in her backpack, but it's for straight hair like Meg's and Mom's. Not masses of curls like mine. I hunt through the bottom of my backpack until I find a rubber band and gather my hair into a clump on the back of my head. While Mom goes to the car to get us clean underwear, I pull the comb gently through Meg's hair, wishing mine were half as smooth as hers.

Meg studies me in the mirror over the sink. "I hope Mommy gets us a real house." A smile tilts up the corners of her mouth. "One that has a yard so I can play right outside our door, and we can have a dog and a cat and a gerbil—maybe even a bunny. I really, really, really want a pet bunny. I really, really do."

The hope in Meg's eyes hits me so hard I have to turn away to keep from bursting into tears. I know that dream of the three of us in our own house, with the white picket fence and the dog and cat and gerbil. It was my dream too, but along the way I traded in fairytale castles for goals big enough to get me somewhere. A big part of my plan is to earn enough money that I never end up like Mom, digging milk money out of a dumpy old sofa.

While Mom drives us across town, Meg and I munch on an apple, trading it between us, and eat crackers we dip into a jar of peanut butter. Meg's school starts before mine, so we go there first.

Mom parks next to the curb in her usual drop-off spot. Meg leans across the seat to give us goodbye kisses before she hops out and yells, "Bye, Mommy! Bye, Mattie!"

Mom and I sit in Ruby and watch Meg walk toward the front door, her pink polka-dot pack bumping against her back. She spent half the night sleeping in a car, yet she marches off to school like it's an ordinary day.

Columbia High School sits on a side street in north Eugene, not far from Meg's school. A one-story brick building, it sprawls back from the road with the gym and auditorium poking up on one side. I hop out of Ruby, grab my pack, and walk to the door, past huge evergreens standing tall and straight like sentinels.

It's my second high school. The first was across town, and you wouldn't think moving to a different school in the same town would be so traumatic, but it was. By the time I started Columbia High, halfway through freshman year, the cliques were well established. Any friends I made were new kids like me. I walk through the door and tighten my grip on the strap of my pack.

Sleeping in my jeans brings a whole new paranoia to showing up at school. In middle school and high school, clothes become this super big deal, especially for girls. Like, if you show up in baggy jeans when the style is ultratight, you'll be labeled a freak, and the sharks will attack, ripping you to shreds before you can scream for help.

I guess it works the same way for guys. If a boy wore khaki pants pulled past his belly button, a dress shirt tucked in all neat and tidy, and anything but flip flops or tennis shoes, he'd probably get beaten up in the boy's locker room.

I weave my way through the halls and do nothing but worry. Do I stink? I hate that. Some people smell, and no matter how nice they are, you don't want to be around them. It's Monday, so at least nobody knows that my jeans and t-shirt are the same ones I wore yesterday.

A tall, gangly guy lounges against my locker, playing games on his phone. I can't squeeze behind him, because the girl in the locker next to me has her boyfriend crawling all over her. I didn't get my morning shower, I'm grumpy from lack of sleep, and I've got a Spanish test hanging over my head like a hammer. I'm in no mood to mess around.

I glare at the guy filling up my space. "That's my locker."

Avoiding boys is the first rung on my climb to the top. Maybe at twenty-five I'll start looking around, but the guy has to have prospects. Education. Money. Plus, he's got to be calm, loving, and stable. All the qualities Mom searches for in a man but never seems to find.

Clear blue eyes flick at me for one nanosecond before going back to his game. I scowl. "I *said* that's my locker. What I *meant* was get out of the way. *Please.*"

The corners of his mouth tip up. He lifts his head and looks at me, making a dramatic tap on the screen with his thumb. Sandy blond hair spills over his forehead with a casual messiness that frames his face. He's handsome. Crazy handsome. But there are bucketloads of boys with such perfect looks your body melts and your breath hangs up in your mouth so much that you can barely talk. It's how they act that counts.

He shoves his phone into the pocket of his jeans, but he doesn't get out of the way. Instead, he folds his long arms across his chest and keeps looking at me. I tilt my head to the side and raise my eyebrows.

His smile spreads. "You're kinda cute."

I sigh and roll my eyes. "And you're kinda in the way."

He still doesn't move. Just grins.

I narrow my eyes, and my voice takes on this razor-sharp edge that's guaranteed to squelch male egos. "I've got class. Now move."

He peels his body off the front of my locker and steps to the side, just far enough for me to squeeze in. His body moves in long, fluid motions, easy and loose. He's tall, like basketball-scholarship kind of tall. "Where's your class?" he asks.

The guy obviously didn't pick up on my get-lost message, so I ignore how close he stands and step up next to him. "Nowhere you need to be."

I open my locker, stuff in my algebra book, and pull out my English papers. The guy shifts his body so he can rest his shoulder against the locker next to mine and study me.

A lot of girls' eyes would sparkle with excitement and anticipation. They would smile and flirt, hoping to impress him enough to snag a date to the next dance or even walk to class with him. Maybe I'm in such a foul mood because I spent half the night sleeping in a car, terrified out of my mind. Or maybe it's that I don't like being the focus of anybody's attention. The real reason, though, is that I won't let myself waste time and energy on boys. Not now, maybe not ever.

I slam my locker door and take off for class. The boy's whole body jerks back, like he didn't expect me to walk away.

I keep moving. He slaps the guy making out with his girlfriend and says, "Later," and falls in step beside me with three quick strides. "Did I creep you out?" I don't respond. "That was supposed to be me flirting."

He leans down, peering into my face. "Was I cocky? Arrogant? Bigheaded?"

"Conceited," I add, making sure not to look at him.

"Brash. Smug."

"Revolting," I throw at him.

"Revolting? Oh, man. Was I that bad?"

He wants me to smile. To say some cute little nonsense thing that lets him off the hook. Girls do it all the time. Smart girls. Going-places girls. Girls of every shape and size. But not me. I extend my stride, but his long legs keep up.

"I'm sorry. I really am." He pauses, waiting for me to respond. "It was stupid of me to come onto you like that."

I don't say a word, but he keeps pushing. "I'm Jack."

Now I'm supposed to giggle, smile, and tell him my name. That's how the whole boy-meets-girl game works, but I don't give out my name to just anybody. My name means too much to me to have people tossing it around without thinking how I feel or who I am. I turn into my classroom without giving him a glance.

I'm halfway across the room when he yells, "And you're not just kinda cute. You're really cute."

I spin around, rooted to the floor with my eyes wide, my mouth hanging open. Jack rests both hands high on the doorframe and leans into the room. The grin on his face spreads to his ears. Twitters of laughter erupt from the class. I turn away, stomp down the aisle, and throw myself into my chair. I could rip off his head.

Class starts and I don't give the locker guy one second of my time. Plenty of boys have noticed me before. Once I show Jack he's not the center of my universe, he'll drift off—like every other boy—and look for a girl that gives him what he wants. I settle into my classes and work on keeping my 4.0 GPA.

At noon, I stand in the cafeteria line to get my free and reduced lunch. That's another part of high school that's hard. Everyone with a shred of extra cash eats off campus. That leaves us poor unfortunates who can't afford McDonald's every day of our lives waiting in line for rubbery hamburgers and slimy hot dogs.

My friend Lilly sits at a table with her boyfriend, Tanner. She waves, and I wave back. Lilly and I came to Columbia High at the same time, so we became friends. We used to eat lunch together and hang out sometimes after school; we even went to a couple of movies and school plays together. Then Tanner asked her out, and that was the end of Lilly and me. We're still friends, but we only talk when we've got a class together or text each other once in a while.

I take my tray to a table, plop down, and prop open my algebra book. High school would be a lot more fun if I had more friends. It's not that I don't like people or can't get to know them. It's just that every time I make a connection, something happens, like Lilly falls in love with Tanner. Or my friend Finn starts smoking weed and hanging out with a bunch of potheads until his mom packs him off to live with his dad. Life seems to get in the way.

I've only gotten one problem done when Jack slides in across from me. He's got a Burger King bag in his hand and a grin on his face that won't quit. I ignore him and go back to my homework. He reaches over and flips up the cover of my notebook so he can read my name.

"Mattie Rollins." He says it soft and slow. Like he's digesting it. Memorizing it. He extends his hand across the table. It's so big he could pick up a basketball one-handed without even straining. "Hi, Mattie Rollins."

The guy's got a calm, easy grace about him, like he's totally comfortable in his skin. Jack leaves his hand hanging between us for way too long, as if he expects me to give in and shake it.

I flick my eyes back to my math book. When he finally pulls it away, I can't keep from glancing up. Jack's face is so soft and open that my heart kind of cramps up before it gets back to a steady thump, thump, thumping.

"Look," I say, "I'll be polite and nice and lay it out straight." I zero in on him so he knows I'm not some sweet, wishy-washy chick who says one thing but means something totally different. "You're wasting your time."

His eyebrows squeeze together so much they wrinkle up his forehead. "You've got a boyfriend?"

I shake my head. "No. It's not that." I try to think of the right words, but my brain is too jumbled. I blurt out the truth. "I've got goals. So I'm not getting sidetracked by some super cute guy with shiny white teeth."

Jack bursts out laughing. He lets the sound flow up through his body and out into the universe, like he doesn't care if the whole wide world knows he's happy. I look around and see that half the cafeteria is watching us. Some of the guys smile, but a lot of the girls glare at me, like I just stepped on their toes or shoved them in the hallway.

Jack keeps grinning while he unpacks his lunch. Two double Whoppers. A huge order of fries. A cup of soda so giant I'd need two hands to lift it. I nibble on my free mac and cheese while he mows through his first Whopper.

He unwraps his second burger, takes a bite, and looks at me across the table. "Fair enough, Mattie Rollins."

He doesn't say another word all the way through the Whopper, so I figure he got the hint and I'm done with him.

"But it's my time." He takes a long slurp of his soda and pops a couple of fries into his mouth. "And I don't think I'm wasting it."

What do I say? Get lost? I already said that, and he didn't seem to get the hint. Before I get another word out of my mouth, Jack points at my lunch tray. "Are you going to eat that?"

I glance at the brown glob of chocolate pudding piled in the corner of my tray and wrinkle my nose. "Seriously?"

He gives me that Oscar-winning smile. "Seriously. I love that stuff."

I push my tray across the table. Jack picks up the plastic spork I used to eat the mac and cheese and digs in. He looks at me, and my stomach feels just like the pudding—all soft and jiggly.

CHAPTER FOUR

"MATTIE ROLLINS," THE INTERCOM CRACKLES over Mr. Zaponski's desk. "Report to the office to be checked out."

Tension drops out of my shoulders, the muscles in my face relax, and relief rushes into my chest. Thank God, Allah, and Buddha too, because Mom must have found us an apartment. She's calling me out of sixth period so Meg and I can get settled before she heads off to work. I slide between the girls in the alto section of the choir, step off the riser, and gather up my backpack. Mr. Z hands me a pass, and I practically skip to the office.

Mom is waiting near the door. She's standing in the shadow of a trophy case that doesn't do anything to disguise the blue-and-purple bruises on her face. I scribble my name on the sign-out sheet and follow her out of the building.

"Is the apartment close? Can Meg and I walk to school, or do we have to take the bus?"

Mom takes off for the door without answering me. That's how I know we're still homeless and sleeping in a car. I don't catch up with her until we're outside tromping through the rain.

"You tried, didn't you?" My words come out loud and harsh, but I'm too cranked up to care. "You didn't just go off to class and forget about us?"

Mom should slap me for talking to her like that. She doesn't deserve any of this—the bruises, split lip, or Darren's bullying. But Mom never hits. No matter how sassy and snotty I get, or how tired and cranky she is, she never turns mean or abusive.

Mom stops in the middle of the sidewalk. "I skipped classes, pounded on doors, and begged apartment managers to take us." Mom holds her arms stiff by her sides, clenching her hands into fists.

"Can't we get a motel?" I say. "Just for the night?" I know I'm acting like a whiny brat, but once I get sassy it's hard to rein myself in.

"No." Mom takes off across the parking lot. "We need first and last month's rent, plus a cleaning deposit. A motel is too expensive."

I'm so focused on Mom finding us a room with a door and bathroom that I walk right through a rain puddle and don't even feel it until my tennis shoes squish out the other side. "What about your friends, Carly or Jen? Did you ask them? One of them could let us crash on their couch for a couple of days, just till we found something."

Mom shakes her head. "Carly's brother and two kids just moved in. That's seven in a tiny two-bedroom apartment."

She stops next to Ruby and opens the driver's side door. "And Jen's husband beats her up all the time. She's finally taking the kids and moving to Portland to live with her mother."

We stare at each other across Ruby's roof. "I'll make more calls, but I can't promise anything. Not for tonight anyway."

Meg hops up and down in the back seat. "We're going to the library, Mattie, and we can read books and do our homework and it will be really, really fun!"

I paste a smile across my face and bat away the worry ripping holes in my gut. We made it through one night on the street, but can we be safe for two? Or is that tempting fate and dropping our odds of survival?

Mom slides into the driver's seat, clutching the steering wheel so hard her hands look like claws. "The library was the only place I could think of where you would be safe." She tilts her head toward a plastic bag on the console between us. "I made sandwiches."

I pick up the bag. Two peanut butter sandwiches along with a baggie of those little carrots. I hand a sandwich back to Meg, pull out one for myself, and take a bite.

Ruby splashes through puddles, her windshield wipers whipping back and forth to clear away the drizzle. Rain is part of living in Oregon, at least in the winter. Some people hate the damp and cold, but I love hearing that soft patter of raindrops on the roof or feeling them plop on my head when I walk outside.

It was easy to love rain when I lived in a warm apartment where I could make a cup of hot chocolate, curl up with a good book, and spend a lazy evening all cozy and dry. Rain takes on a whole new dimension when my home is a car and my tennis shoes are so wet my feet and toes feel like ice cubes.

I force myself to chew the glob of peanut butter in my mouth. We need an apartment. Now. Even a room works as long as we can get to a bathroom. Scrubbing my armpits with a soggy paper towel worked for one day, but we can't keep it up. I choke down another bite of sandwich.

Mom stops in front of the library. I slide out with my backpack clutched in one hand, a peanut butter sandwich in the other. Meg crawls out of her booster seat and stands beside me on the sidewalk.

"I'll meet you in the children's section as soon as I get off work." Mom leans toward us. "And don't let anyone know you're here alone."

Mom searches my face for a sliver of forgiveness. I should give it to her, but I don't. Instead, I turn away and guide Meg to the door of the city library with hours and hours of time to kill. Just like all the other homeless people.

The downtown library is the nicest place we ever go. It's beautiful—three stories high with lots of tall windows and bright open spaces. A glassed-in coffee bar with tables and chairs forms the entryway. The checkout desk is inside by the front door, and across the entry is a wooden staircase that curves around the center, winding up to the two upper floors. All the wood is a natural color that makes the place warm and inviting.

We treat the children's section like a second home. When Darren and his buddies were watching football on his big-screen TV, Mom drove us here to read books and pass the time. We came at other times too, because it's such a great place to relax and hang out. Once in a while, if Mom has enough money to splurge, she buys us a cup of hot chocolate or a cold drink at the coffee bar.

Today, I don't scan the low stacks of picture books, hunting for ones about princesses or animals on exciting adventures.

Instead, I glance around the room, searching for a place where we can spend hours of time and not be noticed. I hold Meg's hand, guiding her past small tables scattered near the librarian's desk. In the back corner, I find a couch, a couple of chairs, and a little round table. If we stay quiet and mind our own business, no one will notice we're here without Mom.

Our first two hours whiz by, but as time ticks off the big clock over the librarian's desk, the minutes slow to a crawl. We do our homework, and I read Meg stories. We take trips to the bathroom, get drinks at the water fountain, and look for new books to read. As the evening drags on, we get tired and hungry.

Meg nestles against me on the couch. "Will Mommy get us a house?"

"I hope so," I whisper. "I sure hope so."

"I miss my dollhouse, Mattie." Meg speaks so quietly I can barely hear her. "Darren better not sell it or give it away or smash it before we get a house, or I'll be really, really mad."

The muscles in my chest constrict, making it hard for me to breathe. Meg's dollhouse, my books, and all the other things we owned are probably gone forever. Do I tell her that or let her go on hoping she'll get everything back from Darren?

Before I can think of what to say, Meg falls asleep with her head on my lap. I gaze at her and stroke the side of her face. My sister is sweet, young, and innocent, but she's strong too. She got tossed into the street and lost most of her toys, and she's still tough enough to stay cheerful and kind.

I ache for Meg, for me, for Mom. Our life wasn't great with Darren, but at least we had a roof and a bathroom. Now all we've got is Ruby.

Mom hurries into the library at five minutes to nine. By then, Meg and I have gone back to the bathroom, gotten drinks, and are standing near the door. I don't need to ask her if we have a warm, safe place to sleep. The dark circles under her eyes and set of her mouth tells me all I need to know.

We park in the same neighborhood we stayed last night. I snuggle deep into our pile of quilts, curl myself around Meg, and hold her tight against me. Reason tells me we aren't the only kids who've spent a couple of nights in a car. It probably happens a lot more than I think, but knowing other kids survive doesn't take away the fear of predators prowling dark, lonely streets.

My mind spins through every horrible thing that could happen to us. The more I try not to think—try to get control of myself—the worse the scenes are that run through my head.

To stop the fear chewing at whatever pitiful bit of courage I own, I say, "Mom?"

Mom sits in the front seat, reading a textbook by flashlight. "Yeah, honey?"

"Do you wish you were rich?" My question sounds all wrong, like I'm some airhead that just wants the latest clothes or fanciest phone. "I mean, what would you do if you had more money? How would you live? What would you do with it?"

Mom clicks off her flashlight, sitting so quietly that all I can hear is her breathing. "I'd get us a house, of course. That would be number one. Not big. Not fancy. Just comfortable, with clean, sturdy furniture, and in a nice neighborhood near good schools."

I'm thinking she's done, that's the end of her dreams, when she says, "And then I'd finish college, so I could get a good job and take better care of you and Meg." She hesitates again and adds, "But that's not the only reason I want to go to school. I hate being ignorant, Mattie. I'm embarrassed that I don't know the meanings of words or the history of our government. People talk about the news, and I don't recognize the countries or their leaders. I want to know things, Mattie. Be educated."

The fierceness she throws into her words startles me. We sit wrapped together in the dark, protected by Ruby's rusty shell.

"What about you, Mattie?" Mom's voice settles back to calm and quiet. "What would you do if we had the money?"

I hesitate too, as if this is the most important question I'll ever answer. "I want the house, the education, the security, but I want to see things too. Paris. London. New York City." I breathe in the cool night air. "I want to hike in the mountains. Swim in a warm ocean. See a ballet. Go to an opera. So much, Mom. I want to do so much."

My mind whirls with possibilities, listing them in no order. Mom and I sit in silence, lost in our own dreams.

"Don't give up those goals." Mom's voice is so soft I can barely hear her. "Hang tight to them, no matter what happens." She leaves the flashlight off, but I don't hear her put away her textbook or pull the quilts up around her shoulders.

I study the rivers of rain gliding down Ruby's windows, tighten my arms, and pull Meg closer. My eyes get heavy and I drift into that in-between space where I'm not asleep, but I'm not awake either. My breathing slows. I sink deeper and deeper into sleep.

Crunch.

My eyes pop open. I peer into the dark.

Crunch.

My breath softens to barely a whisper.

Crunch.

Steps? Someone walking? Rain patters on the roof and muffles sound. I don't move my head but push the quilts aside far enough to peer over the edge. All I see are dark streaks of rain on the window.

I breathe out, slow and steady. I tell myself not to be paranoid. Not everyone is a rapist, murderer, or sex offender. Maybe somebody is walking their dog, or coming home late, or taking an evening stroll. The steps come close, so close they are right next to the car. I don't move, don't breathe, don't even blink.

The steps stop. Is someone bent over Ruby, peering in her windows? Do they see us? I can't see them, but I don't move.

A scream rises in my throat. I press my lips together and lay as still and rigid as stone. Meg sleeps in my arms, but Mom is still awake. I can tell because she is not making the slightest bit of noise, either. We wait, covered in a blanket of darkness.

The person moves on, the crunch of their steps falling away into the rain. I let out my breath. "Mom?" I whisper.

A soft hiss of air escapes from her lips. "Yeah."

"I'm scared." The dark hides my fear and lets me speak words I wouldn't admit in the daylight. "I'm so scared."

"Me too, honey. Me too." I hear tears in her voice, feel them sinking into her sweatshirt, taste them on my own lips. My dreams are gone, lost in the reality of Ruby, parked alone and vulnerable on a dark, lonely city street.

My mind spins for hours or maybe just minutes, conjuring up more disasters. I lay in the damp of the night—scared and worried—until I finally fall asleep.

CHAPTER FIVE

MY LIFE HAS ALWAYS BEEN two separate worlds; it's my method of coping. Like Mom and Meg and whatever living situation we are in is one world, and my school and friends are totally separate. Maybe I keep them apart because I move so much, or maybe it's self-preservation. If people don't know anything about you, they don't have ammunition to use against you.

I walk past the office and head toward junior hall. Racially, Columbia High is pretty much white. Most of the diversity is Hispanic students, but there are a handful of us that are black or Asian. High school is better than the lower grades, though. In some of my elementary schools, I was the only mixed-race kid in the school, and even though I always had friends, I noticed I was different.

I round the corner to my locker bay, and there's Jack, playing games on his phone and leaning on my locker like he belongs there. His buddy isn't around. That means Jack is waiting for me. If I'm honest with myself, I can't say I haven't thought about him in the last twenty-four hours, but I haven't dwelt on him either. Maybe that's because I'm newly homeless, but I don't think so. He's a guy. Just a guy. And I won't let myself get interested.

Jack's busy playing his game, so he doesn't see me. He's got one of those smartphones that can do everything from take professional pictures to offer the latest movies to do half your homework. A phone I ache to own. Mine is a cheap pay-as-you-go model that I'm embarrassed to pull out of my backpack.

For some reason, Jack's phone bugs me more than his being here. It's not that I expect to have the latest technology or envy every new outfit someone wears, it's just the economic spread between the rich and the poor that cuts so deep.

He glances up and spots me standing there looking at him. His face lights up with such joy and excitement that my knees would turn to rubber if I gave him half a chance. Will he stay glued to my locker door, forcing me to beg him to get out of the way? That thought makes me so irritated I'm not prepared when he jumps aside.

"Hey," he says.

I step forward and busy myself with my combination, doing my best to ignore him when all I can think about is my dirty hair and smelly body. I scrubbed my armpits in the gas station sink and lathered on the deodorant, but none of that takes the place of a decent shower.

Worrying about how I smell makes me totally disgusted with myself. If I'm not interested in him, then why am I stressing about whether I stink or not? I keep my arms close to my sides, though, just in case.

"I came by after school," he says, "but you were gone."

I pull out my English book, slam my locker door, and sling my backpack over my shoulder. To look at him, I have to tilt my head up even though I'm pretty average in height. "You're wasting your time. You really are."

With that, I head off to class and mentally tell myself to keep my English book in my backpack so tomorrow I can go right to first period and avoid him. That way, Jack will get tired of hanging around and move on to some other girl who will at least be civil.

Jack falls in beside me in one long, easy stride. "You made that perfectly clear yesterday, Mattie Rollins." He matches his pace to mine and peers down at me as we walk. "But again, it's my time, and I'm determined to get to know you."

I've been mean, rude, and downright nasty, and none of that has discouraged Jack in the least. In fact, the more I push him away, the more interested he gets. I could tell him Mom got beat up by her boyfriend and we spent the last two nights sleeping in a rusty old station wagon. Would that make him uncomfortable enough to leave me alone?

Jack has nice clothes and a fancy phone, plus he's an athlete and obviously popular by the way a lot of guys give him a nod and girls watch him in hope of a tiny flicker of attention. So why is he interested in me—a nobody at this school? I bite the corner of my lip and keep walking.

Jack doesn't utter another word until I'm almost at my classroom door. "See you at lunch, Mattie."

Perfect. He warned me. I can skip lunch and study in the library. The problem with that is I'm starving. Breakfast was a little carton of milk and a couple of those itsy-bitsy doughnuts that sprinkle powdered sugar all over your clothes. Doughnuts that used to be a huge treat for Meg and me, but don't have the same appeal after spending the night in the car. I drop into my desk, furious with myself for letting a guy dictate whether I eat or go hungry.

My English teacher, Mr. Avila, displays a computer screen on the whiteboard. "Here's the outline for your next project."

I'm in honors English, and it's my favorite subject. The workload is more intense, and the books we read are a lot harder than in a regular class. I've always loved stories and I'm learning to like writing—or I at least feel I'm getting better at it.

Mr. Avila points to the screen. "Your job is to write a comparison paper on *Romeo and Juliet.*"

Getting used to the language of Shakespeare with all his flowery phrases was tough, but Mr. Avila had us reading it out loud and kind of acting it. It was fun and gave us all a real feeling for the story. Writing a paper on it will be a snap.

"You will compare Shakespeare's original play with the musical *West Side Story* and a modern film of your choice." He turns to us, grins, and throws up his hands. "I know. I know. *West Side Story* is ancient history, but it's a classic. One you should be familiar with. So rent it and compare it with the play."

My stomach flutters. The TV belonged to Darren. If Mom finds us an apartment, maybe we can go back and get our stuff, but I still won't have a way to watch the movies. I try to calm my stomach, but it doesn't listen and swirls into a tornado of acid.

To stream the films on Mom's computer, I'd need internet, plus Mom's laptop is old and slow and threatens to crash with any extra load you put on it. If I had a decent phone or even enough data, I'd be okay, but not with the cheap plan Mom bought us.

Mr. Avila goes on with his assignment. "The third piece of this project is a modern movie of your choice. Anything with star-crossed lovers will work, but I want details comparing the characters and setting of all three and how they relate to the theme."

I feel sick, like I could throw up milk and powdered sugar doughnuts all over the guy sitting in front of me. It's not that I mind the work. In fact, I like it. It's just that I want the space and time to do my best without life getting in the way and messing me up.

Mr. Avila puts a diagram on the screen. "Pick up this comparison chart on your way out of class. Use it to outline your paper, and I want details, people. Details. This is a big part of your overall grade, and I expect this chart turned in next Tuesday." He grins again. "That's seven days. Seven short days for all you procrastinators."

The tornado in my gut spins around and around, throwing my body into more of a panic than it's already in. Seven days wouldn't be a problem if we still lived at Darren's, but what about now?

The morning slides by. I aced yesterday's Spanish test, which pulls me out of my funk, but then Mrs. Ramon hands us a list of twenty more verbs we need to memorize. By the time I get to chemistry, I've got a plan. As soon as Mom gets an apartment, I'll convince her to buy a cheap TV from the St. Vinnie's store where she got her laptop. They have a ton of outdated technology that still works, and with her discount, I bet we can get something really cheap.

I'm so focused on my workload I totally forget about Jack. That's a lie. I try to forget about Jack and tell myself he won't show up anyway, so why starve myself. At noon, I stride into the cafeteria like I don't care if he's there or not, but my eyes shoot straight for my table. He's there. Waiting for me. This time with a Subway bag.

I could ditch. Take off and leave him sitting there. The smell of sizzling hot hamburgers and greasy french fries makes my knees wobble and my mouth twitch. Jack sees me and waves. He flashes that grin that's too beautiful to look at and makes me forget everything I'm supposed to be doing. I sigh and get in line, knowing if I go hungry or sit at a different table, Jack will grab his Subway bag and follow me.

My butt barely hits the bench before I lay out the rules. "I'm not talking to you. Understand?" I glare into Jack's face. "I've got a ton of work to do, and I'm not wasting my lunch on some pointless conversation that will never go anywhere anyway."

Jack's eyes sparkle back at me and the corner of his mouth pulls up. He holds up a physics book and says, "Agreed."

I pull my algebra book out of my backpack and slap it on the table. Between bites of my hamburger, I work a handful of problems. At first it's hard to concentrate, but once Jack starts scribbling equations in his notebook, I let go of the tension in my shoulders and settle in.

We work through lunch without saying a word. I'm concentrating on my last problem when a man-sized hand slides a giant chocolate chip cookie across the page of my notebook. I jerk my head up.

"I owed you." Jack's face is quiet and serious. "For the pudding."

I look at the cookie. If I take it, am I hooked? Reeled in like some fat, old catfish dumb enough to take the bait? That kind of thinking is ridiculous. Paranoid. It's only a cookie, and Meg would love it. I look back at Jack, but he's busy putting his physics book in his backpack and gathering up his lunch bag.

"Thanks." I slide the cookie back into its paper bag and carefully tuck it into the front pocket of my backpack. "Thanks a lot."

Yesterday, I strode out of the cafeteria trying to ignore the fact that Jack was right behind me. Today, we walk out together. Not like a couple walking all close and snuggly, more like friends. Lilly sees us, makes her eyes extra big and round, and silently mouths the word, "Wow!" I twist up my face and shake my head, like Jack is nothing to me. Lilly grins and rolls her eyes.

In the hall, Jack veers off with a "See you later, Mattie." I head back to my locker and worry that I'm blind, dumb, and steering straight for a cliff.

CHAPTER SIX

THE INTERCOM BLURTS OUT, "MATTIE ROLLINS," right in the middle of my favorite song. Half the choir stumbles to a jagged stop and the other half keeps singing. Mr. Z scowls and waves us to a halt. The message is exactly the same as yesterday. "Please report to the office to be checked out."

I slide out of my section and wait by Mr. Z's desk while he writes my pass. "Your grade is based on participation, Mattie." He hands me the slip. "You know that, don't you?"

I nod, grab my gear, and hurry out of the room. Great. My perfect GPA gets blown to bits with a B in choir. I remind myself to ask Mr. Z for extra credit. Tell him I'll sing an hour every day in the shower—but of course, that's assuming we get an apartment and it's got a shower. How do I pull off extra choir credits in Ruby? Hum myself to sleep every night?

I can tell by the slump of Mom's shoulders we don't have a home. I launch into her before I even sign out. "Choir is graded on participation, Mom." My words spew out in a snotty whine that I hate but fall into anyway. I sign my name on the checkout sheet and follow her out of the office. "I've missed two days in a row." I trail behind her and glare at her back. "Every time I leave class, Mr. Z gives me this sad, pitiful look like I just flushed my grade down the toilet."

The minute we leave the building I let go, my voice shooting up at least ten decibels. "Can't you find anything? Not even a room?" Mom's shoulders hunch, but I don't stop. "Do you realize how hard this is, Mom?"

Mom keeps walking. I want to grab her, spin her around, and make her look me in the eyes. All she gives me to scream at is her back. "Don't you see how tired and sad Meg is? She should be playing with other kids. Having fun."

I wave my hand at Ruby to make my point. Meg sits in the backseat, looking through the window with big, saucerlike eyes. Mom doesn't slow down or even give Ruby a glance.

"Do you even care?"

Mom spins around and yells at me through gritted teeth. "Of course I care!"

I know I should stop, get control of myself, but I can't let go of my anger. "I'm sick of this, Mom. You've got to do something."

Mom slaps her hand against Ruby's roof and yanks open the car door. "What do you want me to do, Mattie? Quit school? Go back to Darren? What if knocking me around or pushing you and Meg isn't enough? How much of a beating do we take before it's too much?" She slides into the car and turns on the ignition.

I throw myself into the front seat and slam my door. "I didn't say I wanted you to go back to Darren."

Mom turns to me, her hands gripping the steering wheel. "Then knock it off. I'm doing the best I can."

Meg clamps her hands over her ears and scrunches up her eyes. "Stop, Mommy. Mattie. Stop." Her words leave Mom and me locked in a stony silence.

Mom drives toward the library while I lean my head against the cold, damp window and stare at the houses sliding by. The good girl side of me lectures in my ear. *You snotty little jerk. Mom is stressed beyond reason. Apologize. Be decent.* I keep my mouth shut. It's not an apology, but it's all I can manage.

Mom hands us our peanut butter sandwiches and drops us off at the library. Meg and I head back to our corner of the children's section like it's our own living room. Meg spreads out her homework on the little round table, bends her head over it, and grips a stubby little pencil in her hand. Soon a row of perfectly formed Gs marches across her lined paper with "Go dog, go," carefully printed along the last two lines.

I sink into the couch. My algebra teacher assigned a ton of homework. I push the fears and worries grinding at me into the deepest, darkest corner of my brain and slam the door on them. I've almost finished my algebra problems when a cute little kid of about six or seven shows up. He's got curly black hair, bright blue eyes, and a mischievous grin. Meg likes him right away. I don't blame her, but he's full of energy and spewing reams of chatter.

He slides into the chair beside Meg and says in a voice way too loud for a library, "Whatcha doin'?"

Meg smiles. "My homework."

I want to tell the kid to scram, but he's not doing anything wrong. He babbles on, asking countless questions and giggling at nothing in particular. Meg shows him her worksheets and the book she's learning to read.

He grabs the book out of her hand. "I can read this!" He starts reading like he's standing in front of a gym full of kids and doesn't want anyone to miss a single word.

"Shhhh." I put my finger to my lips and whisper, "You're in the library."

The little rascal tones down a bit, but his voice still echoes across the room.

I want to clamp my hand over his mouth. Instead, I give him a sweet smile and put one finger back up to my lips. "Whisper."

He stops midsentence. "Why?" His eyes are round with this questioning look that in any other situation would make me want to tousle his hair and chuckle at the sweetness of his face. "I can read real good," he says.

I explain about the library being a quiet place where people come to read, be still, and do their homework. I've almost convinced the kid when I see a librarian coming toward us. My words wad up in the back of my throat and sputter to a stop.

The librarian is short and round, with light brown hair wisping around his head. I want to jump up and snatch Meg away, but that would make us look guilty. Instead, I take the book out of the boy's hand, tuck it into Meg's backpack, and try to ignore the fact we're homeless squatters camping out in the only warm, dry place we can find.

The librarian stops in front of our table. He places his hands on his pudgy, round hips as a soft smile spreads across his face. "Where are your parents, young man?"

I have to hand it to the little fellow. He looks up at the librarian and gives him a smile that would melt a polar ice cap. "Mommy's at work."

The librarian tips his head to the side and raises his eyebrows to make his point. "Then where is your father?"

It's lucky he isn't asking us that question. Meg's dad is getting busted up somewhere on the rodeo circuit, and mine doesn't even know I exist.

"He's using the computer over there." The boy points to the other side of the library. "But I can read real good all by myself."

"You're being too loud, young man." The librarian doesn't quit with the reprimand and keeps right on hammering. "How old are you?"

I put my arm across Meg's shoulders and squat beside her. A cloud of fear mushrooms in my head. This cute kid could land us in the street. Then what? We stand in the cold and dark, waiting for the next five hours until Mom comes back to rescue us?

The boy puffs up his chest and lifts his chin. "I'm seven."

"Well, you're not quite old enough to be in here on your own." The librarian tilts his head to the other side, and stretches his smile so much it turns hard and plastic on his face. "You march right over to your dad now, and I don't want you in here again unless one of your parents is with you."

My stomach ties itself into a knot. The little guy slowly pushes his chair back and stands up. His smile fades. "Bye," he says to Meg with a little wave of his hand.

"Bye," says Meg. "You do read real good for seven."

My mind gallops. Kids have to be a certain age to be here without their parents? Does a big sister count?

The librarian turns his pasted-on smile to me. "Didn't I see you in here yesterday?"

I take a breath to steady my nerves. "Yes, sir. We come to the library a lot."

Then the guy turns to Meg. "How old are you, young lady?"

43

I clutch Meg's shoulder and blurt out, "Eight. She just turned eight." He said seven was "almost" old enough didn't he? Meg is six and small for her age. It will be tough enough to make him believe she's eight, but if I push it to nine or ten, he'll know I'm lying.

The librarian zeros in on me and raises his eyebrows until they disappear into his wispy brown hair. "I asked her, not you."

Meg's voice quivers, barely above a whisper. "Eight?"

"And what grade are you in?"

The guy smiles and acts like he's making conversation, but it comes across like an FBI interrogation. After his last crack, I don't dare answer for Meg, so I squeeze her shoulder three times, hoping she gets the hint.

Meg looks up at him out of the tops of her eyes, her voice stronger this time. "Three? I'm in grade three at Oregon Trail Elementary School?"

My urge is to smile and yell, "Way to go, baby sister," but I keep my face looking like it doesn't matter how old we are, whether we have a bed to sleep in, or a place to take a shower.

"You enjoy the library, girls, but please keep your voices down." The librarian turns and walks back to his desk.

I want to yell at him. "Are you happy? You scared the pants off two little kids and one almost-grown teenager." But I don't. Instead, I lay my head on Meg's shoulder and wait for my stomach to stop churning.

"I lied," Meg whispers in a voice so quiet only I can hear. "Two times."

"You did great. Really great."

"But Mommy says we're not supposed to lie."

"I know, Meg. I know."

CHAPTER SEVEN

'POLICE! WAKE UP!'

I jerk awake, pulling the blankets away from Meg and banging my head on Ruby's roof. Cold November fog wraps us together in a drippy white cocoon. Meg whimpers. I fall back and tuck the quilts around her to keep out the blast of icy air.

The dark shape of a man forms by Mom's window. "Wake up." He raps on the roof. "We've got complaints, people."

Mom shoves aside blankets, books, and white plastic garbage bags. She cracks the window open enough to see the badge on the patrolman's dark blocky chest.

"Police." He holds his identification for Mom to see. "Officer Rodriguez, Ma'am."

Mom slowly rolls down the window. I shiver and tuck the blankets tighter around Meg.

"Your driver's license please?"

Mom fumbles in her backpack until she finds her wallet and pulls out the license. She gives it to the officer without a word.

He studies it and hands it back. "You folks spend the night here?"

Mom takes her license and says, "Yes. Yes, we did."

"We got complaints you've been camping out in the neighborhood."

Mom clamps her arms tight across her chest. "We've moved the car every night."

"Not far enough, Ms. Rollins." Officer Rodriguez leans his hand against Ruby's roof and bends until his face is even with Mom's. Deep creases run down the sides of his dark cheeks, making him look old even though his hair is blacker than mine.

"That shiner's new." He tilts his head to the side. "This guy gonna work you over again? Maybe take it out on the kids?"

A shiver runs down my spine. Would Darren do that? Beat up Meg and me to get back at Mom?

Mom hesitates before shaking her head. "No. We'll be okay."

The officer sighs. "Look, Ma'am. These nice, quiet neighborhoods don't like their streets cluttered up with campers." The lines on his face deepen even more. "They call us, and if we spend our time on the big stuff like murders and rapes and armed robbery and don't get out here to move you on, they go call the mayor and the mayor calls us and then we got to take care of it anyway. Understand?"

Mom nods, but keeps right on staring through Ruby's fogged-over windshield.

Officer Rodriguez bends sideways so he can look back at us. "These two girls your kids?"

"Yes." Mom's voice wobbles.

"What are you doing out here, Ms. Rollins?"

Mom's body recoils, then straightens until she's rigid, like it takes all her strength to hold herself upright. "It's just for a few days." Her voice is soft and tight, fear stabbing at every word.

"A few hours. A few years. It doesn't matter." His face wrinkles into a scowl. "The scum is out there, Ms. Rollins, even in these nice neighborhoods." The lines around his mouth deepen. "You gotta get these girls off the street before something happens to them."

Tears slide down the sides of Mom's cheeks. She doesn't brush them away, just lets them run on and on, dripping off her chin.

"Look, it's not a crime to sleep in your car." Officer Rodriguez slaps his hand on the window ledge. "But you got to have family, friends, something better than this."

"We don't have family." Mom turns to him. "I'm a foster kid. None of my friends can take us in. I've got a job. Two jobs. I can find something in a couple of days. I know I can."

Officer Rodriguez sucks in a breath of air and blows it out in a rush. "That's what they all say, Ma'am." He reaches into the pocket of his jacket and pulls out a folded sheet of paper. "These places can help." He looks back at us. "You get these girls off the street." He taps the paper in Mom's hands. "Now. Before a child molester gets ahold of them."

Shivers roll through me in wave after icy wave. I pull Meg close and bury my face in her hair.

CHAPTER EIGHT

MOM DROPS ME OFF AT the front door of the high school. I've got on fresh clothes and cleaned up in the gas station sink, but I'm still worried I'm a walking stink bomb. I can't smell myself, but it's been three days since I've had a shower or washed my hair.

Jack is standing at my locker. My heart turns cartwheels and refuses to settle down to a steady beat. I stop right in the middle of the hallway. A stream of people flows around me, but I don't budge. I just stand there, angry that my body reacts to him while my mind cries, *Run. Do not stop. No matter how much you want to know this guy. Do not stop!*

"Hey, Mattie."

His words come out soft. Sweet. I don't want to like him. I won't let myself like him. I pull my eyes away, step around him, and open my locker door.

Jack hitches his backpack higher up on his shoulder. "You disappeared again."

I grab my English book out of my locker and slam the door. My intent was to carry it home with me, but Mom pulled me out of choir and I didn't take the time to run and get it.

"I came by after school."

I swing around and look up into his face. "You don't know anything about me."

His eyes are dark and his face serious. "I know, and I'm trying to change that."

Jack does all the right things, says all the right words, and makes it too easy for me to like him.

"I don't want a guy waiting around for me. I don't want a boyfriend. Understand?"

His mouth twitches back and forth, like he's not sure what to think of me. "What about a friend?"

I shake my head and take off for class. "If we were ten that might work." I sigh. "But not now."

Jack falls into step beside me. "We could crank down our hormones and give it a go."

I glance at him. Jack tilts his head to the side, pulls up his shoulders, and flips his hands in such a goofy way that tiny bubbles of laughter ripple through my body, threatening to push my mouth into a smile and force me to erupt into giggles. I clamp my lips together and turn away.

"Not that it would be easy," he mutters, "but at this point, I'll try most anything."

I stop right in the middle of the hall. "Why?"

Jack swings around and stands in front of me. "Why what?"

"Why bother?" I wave my arm. "Look at these girls. Some of them would dump their current boyfriend or even sell their mother into slavery to be your girlfriend, so why bug me?"

Jack's face gets this comical look on it, half serious and half ridiculous. "Am I really bugging you?"

I grip the straps of my backpack and roll my eyes at him. "Don't be cute. Just answer the question."

People push past, bumping into us. Jack sighs. The grin lines on the sides of his mouth smooth out, giving his jaw the square, chiseled look of a man instead of a tall boy. "You're you, Mattie. Straight up. No games." He shrugs his shoulders. "And that lets me be me. Not the prom king or the basketball star or the guy with the fancy new car. With you I'm just an ordinary guy who wants to know this super cute girl with a megasized attitude."

My heart melts into a puddle of raw emotion. I shouldn't have kept up the conversation or asked why he's interested in me if I couldn't handle the answer. Jack doesn't say any more, just falls in step beside me as we drift through the hall to my class.

His "See you later, Mattie" sends another ripple through the pool of my heart, leaving me rubbery and weak. I flop into my desk. This is ridiculous. Insane. I can't waste my time on a boy. Not now. Not for years.

Mr. Avila is well into class before I recover enough to get to work. Three days of being homeless hasn't messed up my grades, but I've got projects coming up and papers due. Stuff you can't work on while you're sitting at a little kid table in the public library or crammed into a dark car. I spend the morning trying to forget Jack and focus on school. By noon, I'm flipping through my workload, putting everything into categories from *THIS IS DUE TOMORROW* to *no sweat I've got all week.*

Jack isn't in the cafeteria. The smart, thinking part of me is relieved; he finally wised up and realized I'm a total waste of his time. Maybe he's even hiding out in the boy's locker room, embarrassed by his sudden burst of honesty. Or maybe he decided he doesn't need the hassle of a person like me, and he's strolling through the hall right now, wrapping some other girl in all the right words and getting more than a scowl and a sassy comeback.

The wishful romantic in me is disappointed. He was a friend. Maybe it was only a three-day relationship, but he knew I existed, seemed like he cared, and was fun to be around even when I acted all snippy and snotty.

I take my tray of pizza and salad over to the table, plop down, and prop open my algebra book. Two tables over, Lilly wrinkles up her face and gives me a look of confusion. She's texted me a ton of times asking for details about Jack, even though I keep telling her there is nothing to report.

I grin at Lilly and shrug my shoulders to either say "I don't care where Jack is" or "I don't know," depending on my mood and her interpretation. She gives me a sideways grin and gets back to feeding Tanner's constant demand for attention.

Despite her obsession with Tanner, Lilly is a good friend, but she lives in a single-wide trailer with her mom, dad, and two little brothers. Just like Mom's friend Carly, her living situation leaves no room for Mom, Meg, and me to crash on the couch. I take a bite of pizza and get to work.

Lunch break is well underway when Jack slips onto the bench across from me. "Sorry I'm late. My parents wanted my latest physics grade." His face is flushed and he's out of breath, like he sprinted through every hallway in the entire school just to get here.

Our eyes lock, and there's no way I can let go. Words of warning shoot through my head. *Careful, Mattie girl. You've got goals. You've got plans. If you fall for this guy you could end up like Mom, pregnant at sixteen and homeless at thirty-three. Be strong, Mattie. Be brave. Be smart.*

I look away and try to focus on my food. It doesn't work. My eyes are like magnets—they snap right back to him, eating up his every word, his every movement. Jack chatters on about his physics grade.

"I've been a lazy bum my whole school career and still managed to keep up my grades." He shrugs. "But it's my senior year and physics is the hardest class I've ever taken. I'm actually doing some homework."

My algebra book sits on the table beside my tray. I can't reach for it. My emotions are too messed up, too conflicted to concentrate on anything but Jack. I should grab my books and run, but the feeling of friendship—true friendship—is so intense I can't let go.

"My whole mission in life is basketball." Jack dips a carrot in ranch dressing and pops it into his mouth. "That sounds shallow and childish, like I'm still a little kid that hasn't gotten past pro ballplayer as my only career option, but I love the game. I really do."

He keeps going like I'm his best friend and he can share anything with me. "I'm not big or tall enough for the NBA, and I don't think I ever will be, but I'm hoping I can land a spot on a decent college team. I don't need the scholarship money, but I really want to play at that level."

Jack throws me another one of his heart-stopping smiles. "And someday, I want to get enough experience to coach college basketball. That's my goal anyway."

I look into his handsome face and wonder how I messed up. How he broke every boy barrier I'd set up.

Jack waves his hand at the tray on the table in front of him. "I'm trying the mac and cheese." He takes a scoop, shovels it in his mouth, and wrinkles up his nose. "Not as good as the boxed stuff." He grins and shoves in another bite. "What's your goal, Mattie?"

"President of the United States." The words slip out of my mouth so easy and quick that I don't have a chance to take them back.

Jack doesn't laugh. He sets his fork down and studies me with serious eyes. "Wow. You do have goals. Big ones. Really big ones."

I've never told a single soul about my dream to change the world. Make it a better place. Help the poor and uneducated and other people in need. I've kept my grand plans secret from Mom and Meg and barely dared dream them myself. Why did I think I could trust them with Jack?

CHAPTER NINE

"MATTIE ROLLINS." THE LOUDSPEAKER BLARES my name for the fourth straight day. "Report to the office to be checked out." Mr. Z drops his chin to his chest and lets his arms flop to his sides. The choir stumbles to a stop.

"Again?" mumbles the girl next to me.

I step off the risers. A guy in the back row yells, "Mr. Z! Write out the pass before class starts so we don't have to stop." Mr. Z scribbles on the notepad, tears a page off, and slaps the pass in my hand.

I need to tell Mr. Z why I miss class, but students are constantly milling around his desk, chattering about concerts and new music or just hanging out. There is never a good opportunity to talk to him alone.

I grab my pass and hurry to the office. Mom is waiting. The minute she sees me coming down the hall, she turns away and heads for the front door. My stomach cramps into a fist-sized knot. She didn't get an apartment. Not even a room. If she had, she'd be smiling at me, even with a split lip and purple bruises on her face. I scribble my name on the sign-out sheet and follow her.

Yesterday, I whined and fussed and sassed like a self-centered brat. Today, I cram all my mean, nasty words into my gut and let them swirl around with the other worries crowding the space. Mom wants a room as much as I do, maybe more. She is halfway across the parking lot by the time I catch up to her.

"Mom?" My voice sounds high and shrill, like I'll break down and cry in the high school parking lot.

Mom shakes her head and won't even look at me. We climb into the car in silence. Meg hops off the backseat, poking her head between the headrests. "When we get our new house, we'll go back to Darren's and get all our stuff, won't we Mommy?"

Mom's body goes totally still, like she's frozen in place.

Meg swings her head over to me. "I'll get my dollhouse and color crayons and story books and Barbie doll clothes, and Mattie, you can get your books and hair brush. And we'll get our beds and all our stuff and the new place will look like Darren's, only better because he won't be there."

Meg doesn't wait for Mom or me to answer. She pops back onto her booster seat and buckles herself in like it's all a sure thing. We'll get an apartment. Meg and I will have our twin beds set side by side with my bookcase in between. All our stuff will be there. Clean. Neat. No Darren. Her picture of life is so simple and clear that my throat swells. I'd cry at the beauty of it all if I dared to believe in something so perfect.

Mom pulls herself together, backs out of the parking lot, and drives toward the library. Meg goes back to playing with her stuffed bunny, while I stare at Ruby's windshield wipers whipping back and forth, clearing away the rain.

Jack is gone, our beautiful lunch shattered by reality. His friendship is nothing more than a dream like Meg's, too perfect to be real. Even if he is ideal for me, I can't have him now. Today, for just a little while, I let myself think I could. I knew better, but I slid into that beautiful, easy space of thinking we could be friends. I soaked up his words and dropped all my defenses. I close my eyes, pushing him out of my head and burying him like I buried all my other childish dreams.

"What was my dad like?" The question slips out of my mouth even though I know the answer. I've asked Mom the same thing a thousand times, but this time I need more than facts. Maybe I need to understand how Mom let herself get pregnant. How she fell for a guy and messed up her life, and how I'm supposed to keep from doing the same thing.

Mom glances across the car, her blue eyes softer, full of relief for my question. She needed to move away from Meg's dream even more than I did. That picture too ideal to be real.

Mom gives me that same sad smile she uses every time she talks about Matt, my dad. "He was tall and slim, Mattie," Mom turns back to focus on the road, "and very handsome, with dark eyes full of strength and kindness and a bit of mischief, just like yours."

She says the same words every time, but they're never enough. I want her to give me a guide for boys. Some bit of knowledge that will tell me which guys are liars and cheats, which are alcoholics and junkies, and which I can trust with my life.

"But was he a nice guy, Mom? Did you love him?"

"He was a very nice guy, but we were kids, Mattie. Younger than you. We liked each other. A lot. And I suppose we loved each other, as much as kids your age can love, but we were just way too young."

"Did you try to find him?"

Mom hesitates, like she does every time she answers that question. "No." She turns down the street and parks in the drop-off zone. I think that's the end of the conversation, but Mom reaches across the car and clasps my arm.

"I should have." She sighs. "By the time I knew you were coming and figured out what to do, he'd moved across the country and the relationship was over." She gives my hand another squeeze. I think she's done—story over—but she says, "I should have found him, Mattie. Keeping you to myself was selfish. Very, very selfish. If Matt knew you were here, he would love you as much as I do."

Tears sting the corners of my eyes. She's never said that. Never told me my dad might have wanted me. Never said what I ached to hear all those years. "Is it too late to find him? Could we at least try?"

Mom studies my face like she's looking straight into my heart. "When we get settled, okay?" She squeezes my hand a little tighter before she lets go and grabs the steering wheel.

Meg and I slide out of the car, stand on the sidewalk in front of the library, and watch Mom drive away. I take a deep breath and blink back tears. My body feels raw, like my skin has been scrubbed just short of bleeding. Love. Hate. Anger. Grief. Worry. Fear. Emotions keep coming, keep beating at me until I wonder how long I can stand them all.

I tighten my grip on Meg's hand. We walk inside, and I steer her across the lobby to the young adult section. Last night's run-in spooked me, so I'm not about to let the children's librarian see us camped out in our little corner for another evening. I find a table by the window, and Meg and I spread out our homework. I drive Jack, my dad and mom, and living in a car—along with all the other junk that pushes at me—right out of my head. It takes too long, but I finally clear my life away enough to concentrate on my schoolwork.

Meg finishes her papers, and when she gets tired, I let her curl up on the window seat with a pile of picture books. It doesn't take long for her to fall asleep. Our spot is perfect, warm and comfortable with an outlet for my phone and a bank of computers close by.

Teens sit in front of computer screens surfing the internet, playing games, and writing school papers. A group of kids huddle around the last computer on the row. One girl glances up at me. Dyed black hair sticks out from under the gray hood of her sweatshirt in short spikes. The girl studies me for a second or two before she focuses back on the computer screen.

I go back to my homework. Honors English is my biggest worry. I make a ton of notes on the original play, but I can't do much more until I watch the two movies. My US History class isn't much better. We're supposed to be working on a PowerPoint presentation on the Civil War, but living in Ruby makes using Mom's computer almost impossible.

I study the kids grouped around the computers. Maybe I could get the PowerPoint done here at the library and email it to my teacher. Could I use them to watch *West Side Story* for English? Do they let you stream films, or do I need a DVD?

The girl in the gray hoodie glances up and catches me staring at them. She steps away from her friends, slips into the chair across from me, and leans her arms on the table. "You're so obvious it's pitiful." Her brown eyes judge me from under heavy black eyeliner.

My mouth drops open, but no words come out.

"You've been sitting here forever, you plugged your phone in where the whole world can see, and you're obviously babysitting." The girl nods at Meg curled up asleep on the window seat, "Is she your sister?"

"Y…yeah, she is," I say.

She rolls her eyes. "You might as well wear a sign around your neck flashing HOMELESS in hot-pink neon."

I glance at the main desk and then over to the smaller information booth. Did a librarian notice us? Are they stomping over here right now, ready to throw Meg and me onto the street?

"Don't worry." The girl gives me a twisted grin. "They're not on to you." She hesitates, glancing over at the woman behind the information desk. "Not yet, anyway. But move every couple of hours or somebody will spot you."

"Will the librarians kick us out?" The thought of standing in the dark in front of the building shoots shivers down my spine.

"They don't care what happens to you. You're a teenager." She nods again at Meg. "But they'll want to know what's going on with your little sister."

"Would they call the police?" My stomach cramps. "Report us?"

The girl shrugs her shoulders. "Like I said, they don't care about you." She tips her head to the side and twists up her mouth. "But you're black and your little sister is white, so people will wonder what's going on."

Heat rises up my neck and flushes my face. "That's not fair." My jaw clenches and my teeth grind together. "Meg's my sister. What does it matter if my skin is browner than hers?"

The girl leans closer. "I'm just saying it raises questions, but that's enough, see?"

Acid swirls in the pit of my gut. Could Mom lose custody of us for being homeless? Officer Rodriguez hinted as much this morning. Meg and I would end up in foster care, or at least Meg would. The peanut butter sandwich in my gut threatens to explode.

"Thanks." I manage a smile even though I can hardly breathe. "I'm Mattie, and my sister is Meg."

The girl doesn't smile back, just studies me with sad eyes. "Ebony."

"Ebony?" My voice flips up at the end. "Is that your real name?"

Ebony scowls. "Don't ask dumb questions."

This girl looks younger than me, but she's got street smarts that make me feel like an ignorant little kid.

I ignore the pain in my stomach and look at the computers. "How do you get to use the computers?"

Ebony points to the librarian at the information desk. "You show them your student ID and library card to set up an account." She glances back at me. "And don't worry. They don't ask for an address."

"Thanks," I say. "Thanks a lot."

She stands up and flicks me a hint of a smile. "Good luck."

Ebony wanders back to her friends at the computer. I look at the clock on the wall behind the information desk. Eight thirty. A half hour before Mom picks us up. I gather my homework, stuff it in my backpack, and wake up Meg. We go to the bathroom, get a drink, and wander through the library. I hunt for spots Meg and I can hang out and not be noticed, just in case we're homeless for another night.

Mom hurries into the library at five minutes to nine. She drives us through a couple of neighborhoods, looking for a spot where we'll be safe, but not obvious. The houses are smaller, more run-down, and much less expensive than the neighborhood where we spent our first three nights. Residential areas feel safer than busy streets, but we have no way of knowing if that's true.

The night is dark, cold, and drizzly. My shoulders droop, and my eyes threaten to close from exhaustion. Mom is tired too. I can tell by the way she hunches over the wheel, like she doesn't have enough energy to hold herself upright.

The neighborhood dwindles to nothing, and we end up in an industrial zone with storage units and businesses of all sorts. The area is quiet and deserted, but is it safe? Are we better off away from other people, or are we more vulnerable?

Mom pulls off the road next to a clump of trees. She kills the motor, and we sit in the dark, listening to the quiet. The trees give me a feeling of privacy and maybe even safety.

Meg whispers in the dark. "Can we make our bed now? Please?"

Mom and I get out of Ruby and open up her rear door. I help Meg flip down the seat while Mom shoves plastic garbage bags aside. Meg kneels in the back and spreads out the quilts.

A car comes around the corner and drives right up behind us, flooding Ruby with light. Mom slams the back down and yells, "Get in the car, Mattie!"

We jump into Ruby and shut her doors. Mom hits the lock button, and the three of us swivel around, trying to see into the light. I expect the headlights to flick off, but they don't. A door slams and the dark shape of a person, outlined by the glare of white light, stalks up to Ruby's side.

"Get out!" The man pounds both fists on Ruby's roof. "My spot. This is my spot."

A gaunt face leans close and stares into the window by Mom's head. Mom and I gasp, too afraid to scream. The guy's eyes are big and wild, his cheeks sunken. The glare of the headlights turns his skin a sickly shade of blue. Raggedy clothes hang on his thin frame, making him look ancient, like a ghost out of a horror movie.

"Move!" he says. Some of his teeth are gone. Others are black and broken. "Move. Now. Move."

Meg whimpers and scoots across Ruby, getting as far away from the man as she can. Mom grabs her backpack and fumbles through it, looking for her keys. She finds them and jams the key in the ignition. Ruby spits and sputters but finally starts up. We drive to one of the neighborhoods we passed and park along the street.

My body trembles. The guy looked and acted like he was crazy, but he didn't hurt us. Was he harmless and just angry because we'd taken his place? Do street people stake out territory like a land claim? This is my bench, my corner to panhandle, my campsite under the bridge.

I understand his need for a space to call his own. If Mom finds us a safe spot to park, I want to go there every night.

There will be a comfort to that, like walking in the door of our apartment. I can relax and go to sleep, knowing I'll wake up to a new day and a new chance to make life better.

We finish making our beds in silence, too frightened to talk. I crawl under the quilts and hold Meg until she finally drifts off to sleep. Only then do I give in to tears, letting them leak out the corners of my eyes and soak silently into my pillow.

CHAPTER TEN

CLICK.

My eyes fly open.

Click.

My every sense leaps into high alert.

Click. Click. Click.

I sit up slowly, my eyes flicking from window to window to window. I expect to see some low-life scumbag peering at me, tapping on the glass, grinning all wild and wicked. Nobody is there. I twist around and there's Mom, crouched in the driver's seat with one hand on the ignition and the other gripping the top of the steering wheel. Her ragged breaths make cloudy little puffs in the cold, damp air.

"Mom?" I whisper. The fuzzy gray of a new day presses tight against Ruby's windows. I scoot up and lean over the front seat. "Are you okay, Mom?"

"Yeah, sweetie." Her words are chopped off, like she has to think about each one before she says it.

"What's wrong?"

She takes her time. "Ruby won't start, baby."

Ruby? Dead? Reality hits me with a thud right in the middle of my chest, crushing me with worry until the very tips of my toes and fingers turn numb and useless. Repairing Ruby costs money, too much money to spare, and what if she can't be fixed? What do we do then?

I shove those fears and worries aside only to have others rush in and take their place. School. Can we walk? Meg will be worn out before we get halfway there. And what about Mom's job? Her classes? Questions spin out of control. I force myself to keep my mind blank, to stop thinking, to concentrate on the little rivers of water sliding down the inside of Ruby's windows.

Mom unlocks Ruby's door, pulls her thin jacket tighter, and steps into the street. She raises the hood of the car. I scramble over the front seat and follow her. Together we peer at the greasy mass of the engine. Cables and hoses snake their way over masses of steel. Nothing in the jumble of parts looks broken, but then none of it makes any sense to me anyway. Riding in cars for sixteen years doesn't give me the tiniest hint of how they work.

"I think it's the battery." Mom wiggles the connections to a dirty black block. "At least I hope that's it." She slides back into the front seat and tries the ignition. Nothing. By now, Meg is awake and asking Mom the same questions I did.

Mom comes back with the kitchen knife we use to spread peanut butter and a pair of pliers from the glove box. She struggles with the pliers and finally pulls off the connections to the battery. Mom scrapes crud off each part with the knife. She puts everything back together, slips into the car, and turns the ignition. Nothing.

Mom and I take turns scraping harder and deeper. Brown flakes drift over the black top of the battery. Mom turns the ignition again and gets nothing but the same dead click.

Meg's voice drifts across the damp, gray air. "I have to go potty, Mommy." She sounds so little and sad. Like being six years old and having to pee is a crime.

I glance around the neighborhood. The houses are small and poor—a totally different community than where we parked the last three nights. Some lawns are trimmed and others are scraggly and long. Any clumps of bushes are set back from the sidewalk and too exposed for a little girl to squat behind.

Panic sets in. Mom grabs her backpack, pulls out her college books, and tosses them on the car seat. I find Meg's shoes and bundle her into her sweatshirt. Mom locks Ruby. She slings her pack over her shoulder but hesitates, glancing up and down the street like she's not sure which way to go. She picks a direction, and we start walking.

Meg clutches Mom's hand and hurries along beside her. "Where are we going, Mommy?"

"To find you a bathroom, baby."

Meg won't last long. I know that by the way she's dancing next to Mom. A car passes. Two dogs bark from behind a chain link fence. A young woman in a baggy sweatshirt, pajama bottoms, and slippers wheels a garbage bin out of her garage. She parks it by the curb and turns back to her house.

I want to ask if we could use her bathroom, but she doesn't look at us. Besides, most people won't let strangers in their house, even in an emergency.

Meg makes it five blocks before she breaks into tears. "I can't wait, Mommy! I can't wait!"

Mom spins around, looking for anything that will hide a little girl's bottom. She picks the biggest clump of weeds she can find, and hurries Meg over to it. She's too late. Before Meg even gets her pants unzipped, pee pours down her legs, soaking her panties, jeans, socks, and shoes. Meg throws her hands over her face and breaks into long, gasping sobs.

"But I'm a big girl, Mommy," she wails. "I'm a really big girl."

Mom kneels in the pee-soaked grass and wraps her arms around Meg. I rub my hand over Meg's hair, aching for her. She lays against Mom's body and cries and cries. Her sobs fill the street and float across the lawns and houses. Her cries finally slow, turning into choking gasps.

Mom struggles to her feet and picks Meg up. My wet, stinky little sister wraps her arms around Mom's neck and her legs around Mom's middle. Mom carries her out of the yard and down the sidewalk. She sets her mouth in a straight line and holds her head high. Pee soaks into her clothes, but none of that worries her.

Mom messed up her life. I've got issues with that. Like how her choices made life so hard for Meg and me. How we struggle just to put clothes on our backs and food in our mouths. But even with all that baggage, I love Mom so much my chest hurts.

We walk for a long time before we get to a main road and spot a string of businesses. I figure we're home free, but there isn't a gas station in sight. In the distance, we see the big yellow arches of McDonald's. It's a long, cold walk, but we finally get there. We head straight for the bathrooms, use the toilets, and clean up as best we can.

Mom herds us out of the restroom. I'm expecting to sneak out the side door without buying anything, but she steers us toward the front. A couple of guys stand in line by the counter. Mom stops, gives Meg a hug, and presses a kiss on the top of her head. "Let's get breakfast, sweetie."

Meg looks up at Mom with big, pleading eyes. "Can't we go back to Ruby?" She glances at the two guys by the counter. "Please, Mommy?"

Mom gives Meg's shoulders a squeeze. "You'll feel better with some hot food."

I whisper in Meg's ear. "No one can tell your jeans are wet." I give her a goofy grin, but Meg doesn't smile back.

We order our food. Hunger gnaws at my stomach, but I think of the money it's costing and don't order as much as I want. We sit in a booth by the window and unwrap our breakfast. I bite into my Egg McMuffin, with its soft melted cheese, real meat and eggs, and warm English muffin, and know for a fact I will never forget the taste no matter how old and snobbish I get. It is the best food I have ever eaten, and I don't mean the best McDonald's—I mean the best food ever.

The last bite of my Egg McMuffin sits in my mouth until every bit of flavor is gone. I finally swallow, knowing I could wolf down two more, drink a giant glass of orange juice, and still be hungry.

I roll up my wrapper, set it on the tray, and glance at the clock on my phone. School has started. Did Jack wait by my locker? Is he sitting in class now, wondering where I am and why I didn't show up? Or am I dreaming? Hoping for this perfect romance that I built up in my head like Meg imagines our sweet little room with all our very own things?

Meg sees me staring at my phone and turns to Mom, her eyes round and full of worry. "Did we miss school? Did it start without me?"

My sadness deepens until it swells up in my chest and forces the air right out of my lungs. I can keep functioning as long as I don't think about anything but the very moment we're living. The minute I look at Meg's stricken face or worry about missing classes, assignments, and all the stuff teachers toss out that you don't pick up if you're not there, my anxiety level cranks up so high I can hardly sit still.

Mom runs her hand over Meg's head, smoothing her long, straight hair. "You'll miss part of it, honey."

Why am I sitting here? I could catch a bus and get to school before I miss any more. I could keep up with my work and meet Jack for lunch. I could even take Meg with me, drop her off, and race to the high school. Mom can deal with the car battery and whatever's wrong with Ruby. She doesn't need me. I ache to go. I itch to take off at a dead run. But I take one look at the bruises on Mom's face, the sorrow in her eyes, and know I can't leave her.

We walk to Walmart and head for the automotive section. Mom and I lift a new car battery into the shopping cart. I'm ready to pay for it and start the long trek back, but Mom veers off to the children's department. I don't get what she's doing and am too nervous about school to care.

"You'll have to walk to the car, Meg," Mom says, "Mattie and I can't carry you because we'll have the battery." Mom stops in front of a table full of little girls' jeans. "I'll get you some dry clothes so you won't get cold."

The jeans are on sale, but the underwear and socks come in packages of three, so Mom has to buy more than Meg needs. The money adds up.

At the last minute, Mom swings by the cosmetics department and walks the aisle until she finds a hairbrush just like my old one. It's a gift, a present I should feel grateful for. Instead, I see dollar signs going up and up and up and our apartment sliding quietly away. In the Walmart bathroom, Mom helps Meg clean up while I brush my hair for the first time in days.

Meg's cheeks glisten with tears. "I'm sorry, Mommy."

"It's not your fault, baby." Mom pulls a comb out of her backpack and runs it through Meg's hair. "If we had a house, none of this would have happened."

The walk back is long and slow. Gray clouds cover the sky. A breeze kicks up brown leaves, but luckily, there is no rain. Meg walks behind in her new clothes while Mom and I carry the double plastic bag with the battery.

"I can get a job, Mom." I struggle down the street, trying hard to walk without banging into the battery between us. The rhythm of our strides has to be precise, or the bag bumps against our legs and makes us stumble. "I could babysit some kid after school at the kid's house and bring Meg along. She'd have fun, and we'd have extra money to put toward an apartment."

Our arms ache and our backs bend at a painful angle, but if we stand up straight, Mom and I are too close and the battery bangs into our shins.

"No, Mattie." Mom shakes her head. "Taking care of Meg is a big enough help."

"I'm sixteen, Mom. It's time I help with money."

Mom sighs. "When we get settled, we can talk about it."

The plastic bags give out and the battery lands with a thud on the sidewalk. The rest of the way back to the car, Mom and I take turns cradling the heavy black block in front of us. The closer we get, the shorter the turns, until we are staggering no more than a block or two before we have to turn it over.

Ruby's dents and rusted paint are such a beautiful sight we burst out cheering when we see her. Mom staggers on until she plunks the battery on Ruby's hood. She lets out a sigh of relief and leans back to rest.

"Get out!" A tall, gray-haired man dressed in baggy brown slacks and a heavy gray sweater stands on the door-step of the nearest house. He thrusts out his arm and points down the street like he's telling a dog to go home. "Go away." The old man throws his anger at us in a thin raspy voice. "Don't you be parking here."

I stand next to Ruby and stare at the old man. He points at us like we're not human. Like we're animals who don't deserve anything but a doghouse or a barn.

Mom quickly sets the new battery on the ground, unlocks Ruby, and tosses in her pack. If that old geezer really wants us to leave, he should come out and help or at least lend us some better tools. Instead, he stands at the door and yells, "This is a nice neighborhood with good people."

The bolts on the old battery are rusted, and the pliers aren't very strong. Mom pushes and tugs and pulls, trying to get the battery loose.

What does he mean by "good people"? Are Mom, Meg, and I bad now that we live in our car? Or does he think I am a bad person because my skin isn't as white as his?

The old man gets cold standing on his front porch. He steps back inside his warm house and stands in front of his giant living room window, glaring out at us. Mom gets the old battery unhooked, and I help her lift it out. We heft the new one in, settling it in place. Mom screws the bolts as best she can.

We climb in, and Mom sits in the driver's seat with her hand on the ignition for several seconds before she works up the courage to turn the key. Dear, sweet Ruby rumbles back to life. Mom lays her head on the steering wheel and cries.

CHAPTER ELEVEN

MOM DROPS ME OFF AT SCHOOL. Fourth period has already started, which means Meg and I missed lunch. Guilt slaps me in the face. I should have thought of that. Should have made Meg a peanut butter sandwich in the car. I was so focused on all the schoolwork I was missing that I never gave food a thought.

I race down the deserted hallways and turn into my locker bay. A brown paper bag is taped to my locker door. I jerk to a stop.

Missed you is printed in bold black marker across the front of the bag. He didn't sign it, but he didn't have to.

I peel the bag off my locker, slide open the top, and peer at a giant chocolate chip cookie. Tears stab at the corners of my eyes. I lean my head against my locker, grit my teeth, and silently tell myself, *DON'T CRY!* I repeat the words over and over and over until my eyes feel normal and I can breathe again.

US History is in the social science wing, which is close. I grab a laptop off the cart near the door, slide into my desk, and flip up the screen. We're researching the Civil War, and it takes me a minute to get my computer up and running. My teacher growls "Tardy," and all I can do is nod. I should have gotten a pass. So what happens when you get a tardy anyway?

By the time class is over, I've settled into seminormalness. I slip the laptop back in the cart and head toward the door. Jack is leaning against the far wall. When he sees me come out of the classroom, his face lights up with such a burst of happiness that my knees turn to jelly. I'm so startled that I stop in the doorway. Students bump and push to get around me.

Why? Why does he like me? I'm homeless. He doesn't know that, but I haven't had a shower in days. My clothes are clean and I scrub my body as much as I can, but my hair is a mass of dirty black frizz.

A guy bumps into me and mutters, "Move it."

Jack meets me halfway across the hall. He throws up his hand like he's taking an oath and says, "Confession. I bribed a friend who works in the office to look up your schedule." His mouth twists, forming wrinkles along the side of his face and across his forehead. "Too pushy? I don't want to scare you away."

I can't keep looking at him. I can't or I'll sink deeper into that sweet, warm place—that place of comfort and peace that creeps up on me every time I'm around him.

I take a deep breath and blurt out, "Thanks for the cookie." I don't tell him that I didn't get lunch or that I had to make myself save half of it for Meg.

Jack laughs. "You're welcome, but is chocolate chip your favorite?" He peers into my face, "You don't seem like an oatmeal raisin kind of girl, but I wondered about the snicker-doodle. All that cinnamon and spice."

I stare into his face and know that if I let myself, I'd like him so much that maybe I could even love him. "It's chocolate. Anything chocolate."

"Except the pudding."

"School pudding isn't real chocolate."

Another easy laugh. "You're right. It's more like pasty brown vanilla."

Words flow right into my mouth. Not like when I talk to most other boys and struggle to think of something to say. The school hallways are too crowded to carry on a conversation, or I'd probably let loose with my whole life history. I stop at my next classroom and we stand there, looking at each other, while swarms of people flow past us.

Jack tilts his head to the side. "Will you be at your locker after school?"

I shake my head and say, "No." Four days ago, I wouldn't have thought of offering him an explanation. Now words dance on the tip of my tongue. I swallow them back.

Jack reaches into his pocket, pulls out a slip of paper, and holds it out to me. "My phone number." His flirting is replaced by a calm stillness. "Call me. Anytime."

I stare at the paper in his hand. It would be so easy to take it. So beautiful to sit in a quiet corner of the library and talk on the phone for hours. I keep my hands at my side, meet his gaze, and shake my head.

Jack looks at the paper, studying it, before shoving it back in his pocket. "And I suppose you won't give me your number, either?"

I let his question hang there between us, unanswered. "Thanks again. The cookie was great." I slip into my classroom and try to ignore the pounding in my heart.

Mom pulls me out of choir, and Mr. Z doesn't even bother with the lecture. Just raises his eyebrows and presses his lips together while he hands me a pass. I keep putting off asking him for extra credit, partly because he's always got a crowd around his desk. The other reason is that I'm afraid Mr. Z will have too many questions about why I leave so much, and I don't want to answer them.

Mom waits by the office, slumped against the trophy case. It's obvious by the way she stands that we don't have a roof over our heads, but all the angry words I've thrown at her are gone, lost in our struggle to keep going. I follow Mom to the car, and we head downtown in silence.

I've only been homeless for four days, and yet camping out at the library seems totally normal, just part of our new after-school routine. Ebony said to hang out in different places instead of always parking in the children or teen sections, so we cruise through the upper two floors, looking for quiet spots to settle in and get comfortable.

Ragtag men slump in soft, cushy chairs, sleeping. They're probably homeless too, just like Meg and me. Old people with gray hair and wrinkled skin sit at study carrels. People of all shapes and sizes cruise through the stacks.

Meg and I pick the magazines section because it is sunny and warm with big tables and plenty of space. Meg chooses some kid magazines to read, and I spread out my homework on the table. When Meg gets tired of the magazines, she digs out her crayons and coloring book.

We've been working at our table for an hour when a guy slides into the chair across from us. "Mind if I sit here?"

The guy is only a couple of years older than me and handsome, with curly dark hair, brown eyes, and the most beautiful long eyelashes I've ever seen on a guy. His face is thin with high cheekbones and smooth skin.

Before I can tell him to scram, Meg grins and says, "We don't mind. The tables are really, really big."

I count five other people in the magazine section and at least that many empty tables. Why does he feel the need to sit here?

The guy wears a blue plaid shirt under a black leather jacket that is soft from wear. He grins at Meg and lays his book on the table. "Thanks." He turns to me. "Doing your homework?"

In a high school cafeteria I'd think he was a regular guy trying to pick me up, so why does his question feel different at the city library? "Yeah," I say. I go back to the algebra problem I'm working on and ignore him.

"How about you little miss," he says to Meg. "Do you go to school too?"

Meg puts her crayon down and gives him her full attention. "Yes, I do. I'm in first grade, and I can read already."

The guy leans across the table and gives Meg a dazzling smile. "Really? Where do you go to school?"

Before Meg can answer, I slam my algebra book shut and reach for her crayons and coloring book. "We've got to go."

Meg's face wrinkles up in confusion. "But, Mattie, we—"

The guy sits back in his chair. "Hey, I've seen you around, and I thought I'd be friendly. You don't have to get all huffy and run off."

His words feel dirty and ugly, like a racial slur even though he may not have meant them that way. I stand up and jam my books and notebook back into my pack. "Let's go, Meg. Now."

Meg starts to protest, but I cram the last of her stuff in her backpack and help her put it on.

"Jeez," says the guy. "What's all the fuss?"

The more he opens his mouth, the more I know we need to leave. I sling my pack on my back and grab Meg's hand. She twists around to look at the guy, but I yank her along. Without thinking, I head downstairs to the children's section. The librarian may spot us, but my bet is Mr. Pushy won't bother us there.

Meg and I find a corner where Meg can curl up and I can finish my homework. I sink onto the couch next to her but don't even open my backpack.

Meg leaves hers on her lap with her arms wrapped around it and doesn't open it either. "Why did we have to leave that boy, Mattie? He was just being nice."

I put my arm around Meg's shoulders and pull her close. "You're right. He didn't say or do anything wrong, so maybe he was just being friendly."

How do I warn Meg about a guy's bad intentions yet not scare her away from everybody who tries to be kind? "When he asked you *where* you went to elementary school, I knew we had to leave, because we never tell a stranger where we live or go to school."

I stop, not sure how much more I should say. "But the most important reason to leave was that I got a bad feeling about him, and that's all it was. Mom calls it the 'creep factor' and says we need to listen to it."

Meg keeps leaning against me. She doesn't say anything, but I can tell she's thinking about what I said. She finally sighs and says, "Oh," kicks off her tennis shoes, and pulls her legs up under her. She opens her pack to get out her school library book and starts to read.

I should finish my last few algebra problems, but my mind and body are too jittery. What did that guy want, anyway? Sex? He was handsome enough to get that some other place. Why approach a teenager and her little sister? Why ask where Meg went to school?

The more I think about him, the more scared I get. Was he trying to pick me up or does he go after little kids? That idea creeps me out so bad, I almost throw up. Meg and I have to be more careful than we've ever been. People that seem nice, like the guy upstairs, could be trying to take advantage of us; people like Ebony, who comes across gruff and mean, are really kind and helpful. The trick is to sort out the difference.

Meg puts her book down, lays her head on the arm of the couch, and falls asleep. I finally wade through the last of my algebra problems and move on to memorizing Spanish verbs. Just before Mom comes, I wake up Meg and we head to the bathroom. I watch the door, and when we're alone we wash our faces with a wet paper towel.

Meg gives me a quirky little grin. "We should put our toothbrushes in our backpacks so we can get ready for bed."

Not a bad idea, until a librarian walks into the bathroom and catches us. Would they care? Or would they report us?

Mom picks us up after work and drives north on Coburg Road, past Beltline, to a set of low office buildings. Even in the dark, I can see the businesses are neat, clean, and well cared for. Trees and shrubs and wide strips of grass separate them from the street and from each other. Two neighborhoods and a homeless camp have kicked us out. Will we have any better luck here?

Mom parks Ruby behind some shrubs so we're not quite so noticeable from the street. She turns off the ignition, and we let the quiet settle down around us.

It's our fifth night in the car, and we've already gotten into a predictable routine. Shove aside bags of clothes. Flip down the back seat. Roll out our blankets. Meg and I snuggle in our nest of quilts, dressed in the same clothes we wore all day. Meg drops right off, but I lay awake and stare into the night. Mom sits in the front seat reading her textbook with a flashlight. The sound of turning pages blends in with Meg's soft breathing.

"Did you love Tucker, Mom?" Tucker is Meg's father. A great dad to me, even after Meg was born.

Mom doesn't answer right away. She's thinking, though. I can tell because she quits turning the pages of her textbook and sits quiet and still.

"I loved him very, very much."

"What happened?"

Mom switches off her light and leans her head back against the seat. The dark wraps around us like a warm, black blanket. "Do you remember when Tucker got thrown off that horse and ended up in the hospital?"

"I remember watching Tucker ride in all those rodeos." I scoot up so I can get a better look at Mom's pale face in the deep shadows of the car. "And traveling all the time with the camper and horse trailer," I say, "and mostly being happy."

"We were happy." Mom sighs. "Until he broke his leg and hurt his back."

I think that's it. That's all the info I'm going to get out of her, but it's like I opened a door she slammed shut four years ago. She tells me how hard she worked to take care of us. How Tucker got hooked on drugs because of the pain, and when the doctors cut him off, he turned to alcohol and street drugs.

"He wouldn't give up riding and wouldn't quit using." Mom's voice chokes. "Not even for us."

I know I'm out of line, but I keep pushing. "And Darren? Did you love him?"

Mom hesitates. "I liked him, and at first that was good enough." She takes a deep breath and blows it out in a rush. "But when he started drinking, it all fell apart. I stayed with him because it was safe and easy, and I thought I could get him to quit." She reaches her hand over the seat and strokes the top of my head. "Don't ever do that, Mattie. Stand on your own. Don't expect a man to fix your problems."

I sink deeper into the quilts and close my eyes. How can I keep from having the same things happen to me that happened to Mom? What makes love turn sour and hurtful? My mind churns through question after question, but I have no answers. Maybe I never will.

CHAPTER TWELVE

I WAKE UP TO ANOTHER cold, drippy morning, snuggle closer to Meg, and pull us deeper into our bed of blankets. Rain taps a sad little song on Ruby's roof, sending trickles of water sliding down her windows. How long can we keep this up? How many nights can we sleep in the car before some psycho breaks a window and drags one of us away?

Mom drives to a truck stop by the freeway where rows and rows of semis fill up a megasized parking lot. Tired looking men move back and forth between their trucks and the convenience store. We could spend the night out here, next to one of these massive rigs, but would it be any safer than camping in a neighborhood or office parking lot? Ruby looks like a Matchbox car next to the triple-trailer semi parked beside us—plus, men are everywhere. We might be in even more danger parked here for the night than on the city streets.

Mom pulls into a space near the main entrance. "Shower time."

I stare out the windshield at the low building in front of us. "At a gas station?"

Meg giggles. "They only have sinks and toilets at gas stations, Mommy."

"Not this one, baby." Mom gives me a poor imitation of a smile. "Two bucks. I called."

We load our packs with clean clothes and troop into the building. The store is crowded, mostly with men like the other gas station, but this one is larger, and has just about everything a person needs. Meg and I follow Mom to the women's restroom through aisles crammed with bags of potato chips and cartons of cookies.

I expect the bathroom to be dirty, but it's not. Clean white tiles surround the sinks, shiny mirrors reflect bright lights, and toilets sparkle. The shower has a small dressing area with a door. It's a little slice of normal.

Mom sets the shampoo and body wash in the shower and hangs our towels on the peg in the dressing area. "We get six minutes."

"Six minutes?" I say. "Is that even possible?"

Mom helps Meg hang her clean clothes up on the pegs. "And we're all going in together."

I stand outside the dressing room door, staring at her. "What?"

Meg claps her hands and giggles. "Come on, Mattie. It'll be fun."

Meg takes showers with Mom all the time. I used to, until I grew up. Mom shoots me a steely look, and I know I can either climb in or go stinky.

We strip down and huddle together in the tiny dressing area while Mom gets everything set. She drops coins in the slot, turns the lever, and water blasts into the stall. She wastes a couple of seconds getting the temperature right, but when she does, we all crowd in.

Meg giggles while she rubs body wash over my back. Mom shampoos Meg's hair. I lather mine up and start in on Mom's. We work fast, rinsing the shampoo out of our hair before we scrub our bodies. The water keeps running, and I even have a few seconds to enjoy the warmth before the timer gives a loud clunk and the water shuts off.

I'm clean. In six minutes, with two other people crowded in beside me, I get clean. We dry our hair under the hand dryer by the sink. For breakfast, Mom buys a small carton of milk and cereal in those little plastic tubs. We eat breakfast in the car, and by the time she drops us off at school, I feel almost normal.

I practically bounce through the front door of Columbia High, and I am halfway to my locker when I spot Ebony's spiky black hair across the hall. Her leather jacket, t-shirt, jeans, and heavy boots that lace up to her knees are all black to match her hair and eye makeup. I veer toward her, but she stops me with a look. On another day, I might have been hurt, but today, I get it. Ebony's carefully constructed her life and doesn't need me to mess it up.

I keep walking and swing into junior hall thinking my life may not be great, but at least I don't stink. I turn into my locker bay, and there's Jack leaning back on my locker playing games on his phone. My face breaks into a smile—no matter how hard I try, I can't wipe it off.

Jack sees me and jumps away from my locker. "Hey."

We stand there, grinning at each other.

Jack steps closer. "I really missed you."

The words "I missed you too" bubble up. I manage to clamp my lips together to keep them from shooting right out of my mouth. I finally pull my eyes away from Jack and turn to my locker.

Jack's buddy is back, this time pressing up against the girl at the locker next to mine, nuzzling her neck and kissing her hair. She giggles, wiggles, and coos while his hand slips up the back of her sweater. If that jerk tried touching me, I'd break every finger he owns. But what if Jack kissed my neck and held me like that? What if his hand slid over my body, touching my bare skin?

Heat waves flash through me, turning my face hot and my palms sweaty. I spin the dial of my lock, but my hands are so damp I have trouble with the combination. Jack doesn't say anything, just leans his shoulder against the opposite locker and watches me. I pull my English book out from under a pile of papers, stuff it in my backpack, and slam the door. Jack's friend uses the jolt to slide his hand up a couple more inches.

The fire raging through my body makes my heart beat so fast I feel dizzy. I don't dare look at Jack. Don't dare walk next to him. I back away and take off for class, kicking myself for being so foolish. No boys. That's rule number one. A guide I've got to live by. It's the only way I'll ever be anything but poor.

Jack falls in beside me. "You're mad." He keeps up with me, but his body turns my way and his eyes study me. "Did I say something stupid? Do something weird?"

This makes me stop midstream, and a couple of people bump into me. "I am mad." I look up at Jack. "Mad at you. Mad at me."

Jack stops, wrinkles up his forehead, and peers down at me. "Why? What did I do?"

I flip my hand out and point my thumb back toward my locker. "That guy." I roll my eyes. "The one crawling all over his girlfriend?"

Jack glances back toward my locker, shrugs his shoulders, and looks back at me. "What about him?"

I stare up into Jack's eyes and know I'm not making sense. I try again. "I can't have a boyfriend." I look away. "I told you that."

Jack leans close. "So I didn't mess up?"

His words are soft and almost whispered, making it impossible not to look at him. Jack's face is so full of confusion and worry that it holds me there. Even though I know I should take off at a dead run, I can't move. "No. You didn't mess up."

I bite my lip and look away again. "I get scared." Why do words slide right out of my mouth like I'm reading them in a book instead of living them? Why do I tell Jack things I don't even admit to myself?

Jack sighs. "Jeez, Mattie," he whispers, "I'm scared too."

We walk the rest of the way to my classroom in silence. I turn into the room, but Jack grabs my hand and holds me back. "We can talk about stuff, Mattie. We really can."

His touch sends bolts of electricity shooting through me, setting me on fire and melting me with its heat. I pull my hand away and hurry into class.

All morning I question my sanity. One minute I think I can handle the thing with Jack and me, and the next minute I know I can't. At noon, I head straight to the cafeteria, telling myself to toughen up and get over this stupid attraction to a guy that happens to say and do all the right things. Mom got into her mess of a life by listening to good-looking, sweet-talking guys, and I'm not going to do the same thing.

Jack is waiting by the door. He sees me and flashes that grin. My heart does a little pitter-patter before I slam a lid on it. Without a word, he drops in line behind me. I jerk a tray off the stack and slide it along until I'm in front of the hot dogs. The kitchen worker drops one on my tray.

Jack leans toward me and whispers, "Why the hot dog and not the hamburger?"

I glance up at him. "Hot dogs aren't real meat anyway, so you're never disappointed." I try to be blunt, say it like he means nothing to me, but it doesn't work. He knows I care. I can see it in his eyes.

Jack laughs and asks the cafeteria worker for three of them. My resolve to ignore him fizzles. Just sputters right out in that infectious laugh of his.

Lilly gives me a thumbs-up from across the cafeteria. I try to roll my eyes and act like Jack doesn't mean a thing to me, but instead, my mouth tips up in a corny excuse for a smile.

Jack slides in on one side of "our" table, and I slide in on the other. My algebra book emits guilty vibes, telling me to get going and do my homework, but I tell myself eating a mustardy hotdog will put yellow smears all over my math paper. That's my excuse anyway.

Jack dips his hotdog in ketchup and then mustard. "Tell me about your family." He studies me while he bites a massive chunk off the end.

There it is, that probing, personal question that you don't want to answer. I hesitate. "There's just three of us," I say. "Mom, me, and my little sister, Meg." Safe. He doesn't know we're homeless, or that Mom's face has purple bruises and a split lip.

"You're lucky to have a sister." Jack polishes off the first hotdog in one last bite and picks up the second. "I'm an only child, which makes me spoiled rotten." He wiggles his head back and forth. "Name it, and Mom and Dad buy it."

I snort. "You have a car?"

Jack's face goes all tight and still. "Actually, two. Dad bought me a little Honda for running around town, plus our family has an old four-wheel drive Jeep I use for skiing and anything else I want to do. They never drive it, so it's basically mine." He glances away, embarrassed.

My mouth drops open, and my eyebrows shoot up my forehead. He's not some regular kid who has nice clothes and doesn't have to worry about lunch money. Compared to most kids' standards, he's rich.

"Two cars?" I drag the words out super long, which only embarrasses him more.

Jack tips up one shoulder in an offhand shrug and turns back to me. "How old is your little sister?"

Meg is the one part of my life I can be totally honest about. I don't mean to let it happen, but words spill out, tumbling over and over each other. I tell him how she dresses up as a different princess every year for Halloween, that she loves to play with her dolls and stuffed animals, and that she has this happy disposition that makes it easy to love her. I tell him how proud I am of her reading, and how hard she tries to learn new things. Our lunch is long gone, and we're still sitting there.

"Mom's a single parent, so life's a struggle." Which is a total understatement, but at least I didn't lie. "I need to get through college and make good money so I can help Meg go to school too." My last words hang in the air between us, exposing half my soul. "I'm blabbering."

Jack wrinkles up his face. "Conversing."

I close my eyes and shake my head. "Prattling."

"Sharing."

I look straight at him. "I never drivel on like that."

The corner of his mouth twitches. "I know. That's one of the reasons I like you."

Raw emotion. That's me. A jumble of nerves and hormones and electrical charges all stuffed in my body waiting to explode. We walk back to class, and I might as well be strutting down the halls naked. That's how scared I am.

CHAPTER THIRTEEN

SIXTH PERIOD. MR. Z GLANCES up just as I walk into the choir room. "Mattie," he says, waving me over to his desk. "I need to see you."

I clutch the straps of my backpack and walk over to his desk. Did my grade drop to a B? Is that what Mr. Z wants to tell me? Could a B in choir ruin my chances for a college scholarship?

I should tell him why I leave class every day, but a bunch of guys are hanging close to his desk. They'll hear me spill my pitiful tale of woe, and who knows what kind of snide remark that would bring.

Mr. Z hands me a pass. "I'm guessing you don't have a choice to leave class." He picks a piece of paper up off his desk. "So write me a decent paper on this topic and you can hang on to your grade."

Tears stab the corners of my eyes. I blink them away, press my lips together, and glance at the words he's written. History of Jazz—at least five pages with references—due by the end of the term.

I clutch the paper in my hand. "Thanks, Mr. Z. Thanks a lot."

Halfway through class, the intercom announces, "Mattie Rollins. Please report to the office to be checked out." Mr. Z doesn't even look my way. He just keeps right on directing, and the choir doesn't miss a note as I step off the risers, grab my backpack, and head for the office. I scribble my name on the sign-out sheet and follow Mom out the door. Mom drives us back to the library.

Meg and I troop in past a crowd of kids in the coffee kiosk and head upstairs to the second floor. I avoid the magazine section and steer us through adult fiction until I find a quiet little table in the back. We haven't hung out here before, so I feel safe, yet hidden from Mr. Pushy or any other prying eyes. Meg practices her writing while I concentrate on finishing my algebra and Spanish homework.

When I'm done, we head downstairs to the information booth by the young adult section. Asking the librarian the simplest of questions feels like I'm shouting HOMELESS and will put Meg, Mom, and me into a bad situation. Getting an alternate assignment from my teacher does the same thing. Even if I lie and make up some story about how our TV and computer are broken, it doesn't change the fact that most kids have a neighbor or friend they can turn to. I shouldn't be afraid, because the librarian's job is to help people, but I still have to take a deep breath and work up my courage before I can speak.

"Hi," I say. "I need to use a computer for a school project. Could you help me?"

The older woman behind the desk is tall and thin with soft gray hair. She looks up at me with hazel-brown eyes and smiles in a way that makes me wonder why I put off getting help for so long.

"I'd be happy to," she says.

I explain my movie project for English and the PowerPoint presentation I need to do for US History.

"No problem," says the librarian. "I'll show you all you need to know."

The woman takes me over to an empty terminal. Meg follows along. I sit down, and the woman walks me through everything I need to know. She shows me how to access PowerPoint and where to put a movie disc, then hands me a headset. It's all so easy that I'm embarrassed I stressed about it.

"Thanks," I say. "Thanks a lot."

"No worries," she says. "Come get me if you have any trouble."

Meg settles into the window seat with a pile of picture books she wants to check out. I look around for Ebony, but I don't see her. I miss her, even though I don't even know her.

My PowerPoint presentation is all mapped out. I input the data and look for pictures and graphics to download, working until I'm happy with the result. I save it online so I can fine-tune it before I send it to my teacher. *West Side Story* is on a disc here at the library, so tomorrow I'll watch it, take notes, and find another film for Sunday. My homework is coming together so well I almost feel happy.

Meg is sleeping on the bench with her head leaning against the window and a blanket of books spread over her tummy. Who do I think I'm fooling? Ebony is right. I'm black and Meg is white. Every librarian in the building knows that we've spent five evenings in a row camped out here. We can try to stay hidden, but by now, they've all seen us and remember us.

Mom picks us up, and we go back to the office parking lot to camp out. I burrow into our bed tight against Meg, pulling the quilts up around our faces. Black surrounds us and calms me so much my mind drifts to Jack. I see his grin and hear his infectious laugh. I marvel at how he makes me smile, even when I don't want to. Every moment, every word we've shared slides through my head.

Worry drifts away and leaves me with tiny pinpricks of hope. Am I being foolish? Blind to the problems of a relationship? I shove thoughts of him away. Daydreaming about Jack floods me with emotions I can't handle, at least not now. I fall asleep wrestling with my heart, my head, and my hormones.

I wake up startled and afraid for no reason. Was I deep in a dream that I don't remember? Is that why sweat makes my hands cold and my face clammy?

Highway traffic hums in the distance. I lay in the dark, listening to Meg's slow, steady breathing. I open my eyes, push the quilt back, and scoot up on my elbow. Headlights cruise across the parking lot, heading straight for us.

Cops? We've dealt with them before. It isn't a crime to park on the street, but what about an office parking lot? Mom locked Ruby's doors, so I tell myself not to be scared. We're safe as long as we've got Ruby. The headlights pull up right behind us, flooding us with a bright white glare. Doors slam.

Someone calls, "Check out this piece of junk."

The lights blind me, making the rest of the world impossible to see.

"Hey, look. There's somebody inside."

It isn't the cops.

"Look. It's a lady. Maybe two."

A pale face presses against the side window right in front of me. A scream rises in my throat. I jam wads of quilt against my mouth to muffle my fear. A hideous grin spreads across the face.

"Hey there, sweetheart."

Meg pops up beside me. "Mattie?" I push her under the quilts, covering her mouth with my hand and whispering in her ear. "Shhhhh. They won't know you're here."

The guy presses his lips against the window in a slimy imitation of a kiss. "Party time, girls."

"Mom." I whisper. "Get us out of here."

Mom rips off the quilts wrapped tight around her body. She shoves them onto the passenger seat with our plastic bags of clothes, grabs her pack, and frantically digs through the front pocket for her keys. A dark form grabs Mom's door handle, yanking it hard enough to rattle the metal. "Open up."

Three more faces peer into Ruby's fogged-over windows. Hands grab her door handles, rocking us back and forth on her tires. "Come on out, girls. It's party time."

Mom's hands are shaking so much she's having trouble getting the key in the ignition. Meg trembles in my arms, her fear so intense I can taste it.

"Mom!" I yell. "Get going!"

Mom turns the key. Ruby's engine rumbles to life. I suck in a lungful of air, so grateful for Ruby's new battery that tears spring to my eyes. Mom pops on the lights. That's when I know we're trapped.

Laughter erupts all around us. A guy leans close to Mom's window and gives her a twisted grin. "Oops."

Ruby's headlights shine on the grass, trees, and shrubs of a median strip stretched out in front of us. Our taillights outline a car parked so close behind we can't back around it.

The man keeps peering into the window, inches from Mom's face. "You ain't goin' nowhere, pretty thing, so come on out and enjoy yourself."

"Do something, Mom!" I yell.

The men start rocking Ruby back and forth, back and forth.

"We'll wreck the car." Mom's words bounce around the interior, hitting windows, doors, seats and reminding us how desperately we depend on Ruby.

The face at Mom's window disappears. The tension in my neck and shoulders starts to ease, but before I can catch my breath, the man comes back. This time, he holds a baseball bat. "Open the car door, missy, or you'll wish you had."

The guy's weapon sends long fingers of fear into my chest. "Go!" I scream. "Go!"

Mom revs the engine. "Hang on." She throws Ruby into reverse, and the laughter outside our windows changes to shock and anger. Ruby flies backward, shattering taillights and headlights and crumpling fenders. Voices yell obscenities, and beer bottles crash against our side.

I hold on to Meg, grit my teeth, and brace my legs.

Mom throws Ruby into drive but not fast enough. The guy with the baseball bat connects with the driver's side window right next to Mom's head. The glass shatters in a honeycomb of cracks, sending crumbles spraying through the car.

Mom slams her foot down on the gas, and Ruby shoots forward, lurches over the cement curb with a nasty scrape, slides across grass, and crashes through shrubs. Mom keeps her foot to the floor, spins the wheel, and churns through the turf. She jerks the wheel again, and we bump back onto the pavement, scraping along the edge of the curb.

Beer bottles pelt us. The men yell strings of ugly words. I should cover Meg's ears, but I can't shift positions or we'll be thrown back and forth against the side of the car. Mom guns the engine, and Ruby's front end skews wildly out of control. Mom straightens us out, races through the parking lot, and drives into the street.

I loosen my grip and let my legs relax, thinking we made it—terrified but safe. Mom knows better. She yells, "Put the seat up!" Her eyes never leave the road. All her concentration is zeroed in on driving as fast as she dares. "Buckle in and hang on."

Cold wind from Mom's broken window whips through the car. Chills run up and down my spine, but it's not just from the cold. The broken window takes away any shred of protection we had.

I let go of Meg and shove our blankets and pillows to the rear of the car. Ruby swings and sways, but I finally get the back seat pulled up and locked into place. Headlights flood us with a blinding bright glare. Meg climbs over and buckles into the back seat. The car behind us eats up our head start with frightening speed. I slide over the top of the seat and buckle myself in.

Mom races down the street while I keep watch out the rear window. Where can we go? It's the middle of the night. Businesses and public buildings are closed. Homes are dark.

"If they force me to stop, take Meg and run. Understand?"

"No, Mommy," sobs Meg.

My breath freezes in my throat. "I'm not leaving you."

"Don't argue." Mom's eyes never leave the road, but

I don't have to look at her to feel her fear. "Run. Bang on doors. Call 911." When I don't respond, Mom screams at me. "Promise me!"

My mouth is too dry to answer.

"Mattie!"

"Okay, Mom." My words come out strangled and choked. "I promise."

"Start looking for places to go. Meg, you look too."

Mom flies through a red light, swings south on Coburg Road, and drives too fast for city streets. The car follows so close I think they'll ram us. Mom pushes Ruby even faster. The car slides up beside us, threatening to force us off the road. I focus on the buildings whizzing by, looking for a safe place to run. Houses. Parks. Stores. All dark.

We speed through town, ignoring stop signs and traffic lights. I pray for the red and blue flashes of a police car. There isn't one in sight. Mom turns a corner too fast, and Ruby rocks on two wheels. She speeds block after block down narrow streets, whips around corners, and pulls into a parking space right in front of the city police station. The car behind us slows to a crawl. Four angry men hang their heads out the windows and yell at us, polluting the air with their filth.

Bright lights above the police station door wash over Ruby, casting us all in an eerie yellow glow. Mom and Meg and me sit in a trance, silent and alone, expecting the men to sneak up on us, our escape turning into nothing more than a delay. Mom finally turns off the ignition, and her head slumps forward. Her shoulders shake. Deep sobs rip at her body. Fear fills every inch of our battered and beaten Ruby.

Meg and I fall asleep sitting up, wrapped in quilts and slumped against the doors. I don't think Mom sleeps at all.

CHAPTER FOURTEEN

A SLAP ON RUBY'S HOOD jolts me awake and throws my heart rate into overdrive. Mom screams, Meg starts crying, and I try to slow the pounding in my chest long enough to focus.

A voice mutters, "Did he find you, Ms. Rollins? Beat up the car? Is that what happened? Did he work you over again—or beat on the girls?"

Officer Rodriguez leans one hand against Ruby's roof and picks bits of glass out of Mom's window frame. His broad face looks even angrier than when we saw him before. "Your taillights are broken, your back bumper looks like you took on a Mack truck, and now you can't even lock the doors."

Last time Officer Rodriguez talked to us, Mom barely said a word. This time, she tells him about the assault on Ruby and how we barely got away; she throws in how safe she thought the office parking lot would be and adds how Ruby's dead battery cost us a ton of money. Her words spill over each other, faster and faster, until our whole pitiful lives are laid bare.

The officer listens, but the anger on his face only deepens. "Did you check that list of services?"

"Two shelters are full and the others don't take kids." Mom stops and takes a deep, shuddering breath. "I work two jobs and go to college. I can pay for housing if I could just get the deposits together and find a room we can afford."

"You gotta get off the street." Officer Rodriguez leans closer, with one hand resting on Mom's window frame and the other on Ruby's roof. "You got lucky, but next time these kids could get hurt." He pauses, glancing back at us. "Then the state's got to step in to protect them." The wrinkle lines around the officer's mouth soften and he looks back at Mom. "You don't want to lose your kids, Ms. Rollins. I know you don't."

Mom presses her hand to her mouth, but little sobs bubble out anyway, spilling into the car and filling every square inch of space with worry and despair. Meg lays her head against Mom's shoulder, offering the soothing comfort of a six-year-old. I reach over the seat and squeeze Mom's shoulder. Her bones feel sharp and hard against my hand.

Officer Rodriguez stands up and watches a couple of cars glide by. He takes a notebook out of his pocket, writing in quick little bursts. Mom pulls herself together, lifts her head, and wipes away the tears with the backs of her hands.

The officer squats down by the car, notebook in his hand. "The perps' main line of mischief was probably theft, but when they saw you, they decided to have a little fun. Give me the details. I'm headed into work, anyway."

"Four guys," I blurt out, "but there could be one more. I definitely saw at least four."

He glances at me. "Color of car?"

"Dark. Couldn't tell the color, but the front end has plenty of damage." I study his face. "Mom rammed 'em pretty hard."

"I bet she did." He sticks his notebook in the inside pocket of his jacket. "Fix the window and the taillights as quick as possible. Understand?"

Officer Rodriguez slaps his hands on the window ledge. "And use hand signals, or somebody could rear-end you. It's Saturday, so most garages are closed, but if you find one open and they say they're booked, tell them I sent you. Can't guarantee it'll get you in, though."

Mom nods, her cheeks glistening with tears.

I lean forward and look into the officer's face. "Check the beer bottles for fingerprints. They threw a bunch, and if you go back to the parking lot, you might get a print."

He turns to me. "We might just do that." He stands up and rests his hands on the roof of the car. "Get off the street, Ms. Rollins. Pick a shelter. Get your name on a list for affordable housing. Go to the Mission. Just get off the street."

Officer Rodriguez walks away, and Ruby suddenly feels empty, like Mom, Meg, and I are sitting in a black hole with no way out. We might as well be lost and alone in a maze with every turn we make ending up all wrong.

We sit there and stare into space, drained of emotion. No talking. No discussion about what we do next or how we survive. We just sit there. Our life is falling apart, little bit by little bit. Money dribbles away. First a car battery. Now a window and taillights. It's like the longer we're on the street, the harder it is to save enough money for a room, much less an apartment.

Mom finally leans forward and turns the ignition. Ruby runs. She rattles and shimmies, and the cold breeze rushes through her broken window, but she works. For that, I am grateful. Life with her is scary enough—life without her is too horrifying to consider.

Mom drives to the gas station. She grips the steering wheel so tight her fingers look white and dead. We go to the bathroom, clean up, and eat peanut butter sandwiches for breakfast. On Saturdays, Mom works eight to five at 7-Eleven. We need the money, so she has to go, even though she's so shaken up she can barely stand.

"The library opens at ten." Mom's words come out all flat and hollow, like she doesn't dare put one bit of emotion in them or she'll break in half. "You'll have to stay in the car for a couple of hours, then take the bus downtown."

Spending two hours sitting in Ruby, looking over our shoulder for the parking lot scum to find us, sounds scary, but also incredibly boring.

"I'll park out front." Mom's voice wobbles. "I'm not supposed to, but it's not for long."

"What about tonight, Mom?"

She doesn't answer, just stares through the windshield with a hollow look.

"Mom?"

She screws up her face and bites her bottom lip. "I'll call the Mission and see if we can get in."

My shoulders drop six inches, or that's how my immense sense of relief feels. I don't know where the Mission is or what it's like, but I don't care. We've got to go.

Mom drives so slowly through the streets it's like she's making up for last night's road race. I don't mind. Moving feels good, like no one can get to us as long as we keep Ruby running.

"Meg and I could go to the mall." Doing something other than hanging out at the library chases away a small bit of my anxiety. I hurry on with my plan before Mom can cut me off. "We could hang out for a while and take a bus to the library in the afternoon."

Meg's head pops up and her hands clap together. "Please, Mommy? Can we?"

Mom doesn't look at us. "None of the garages are open yet, so I'll have to find one and take Ruby during my morning break."

"Mom? The mall?" I say.

Mom turns to me with a blank stare. She didn't hear a word I said—or at least it didn't register.

"Please, Mommy. I love the mall." Meg claps her hands and leans forward. "We get so tired of staying at the library."

Mom turns her attention back to the road, driving several blocks before she answers. "You'll have to figure out the bus."

"We can do that."

"Please let us," says Meg. "Please?"

Mom is too upset to argue. She parks right in front of the 7-Eleven, grabs her backpack, and digs through it until she finds her wallet. She pulls out five one-dollar bills for bus fare and hands them over to me. Before she heads to work, she gives us each a long, teary hug and a hard kiss on the top of our heads.

I make more peanut butter sandwiches and read Meg a bunch of stories before I decide it's time to go. Meg and I walk to the bus stop and wait. Standing on the side of the street with cars rushing by makes me nervous. I clutch Meg's hand and study every car, looking for dark colors and smashed-in front ends until our bus rumbles up. Meg and I hurry up the steps, settling into the warmth and safety of its blue plastic seats.

We ride to the downtown station, the central hub for all the busses in Eugene. It's right across the street from the library and a busy place, with a narrow metal roof covering the walkway and benches underneath. Each bus pulls up parallel with the sidewalk to where a sign marks the run and gives departure times.

Meg and I step off the bus and head to the map on the wall near the office. We find the route to the mall, walk back to the correct bus stop, and wait until it shows up. Our trip isn't hard, but it does take time. Even with the delay, we arrive at the mall way too early. The main doors are open, but giant metal grates block entrances to the stores. Meg and I drift past handfuls of early morning shoppers, sipping from their Starbucks cups and waiting to spend their money.

Girls at school talk about shopping at the mall all the time. From the way they brag, their parents buy them piles of clothes throughout the year; they get new outfits for Christmas parties or school dances, or just because they want them. Girls admire each other's purchases and chatter about where they shop and what good deals they find. Meg and I hardly ever go to the mall. Any new clothes we get—usually shoes, underwear, and socks—come from discount stores like Walmart.

Meg points to the windows of a big department store. "They got Christmas stuff out."

"It seems early." I'm startled by how much my words sound like Mom.

"Thanksgiving comes first," says Meg, "and *then* we get Christmas."

We stop in front of a window display with fake snow on the ground and plastic kids in warm winter coats. The plastic girls with no faces wear pink and lavender and baby blue with striped hats, scarves, and mittens, all in perfect, matching colors. The boys wear bright red and blue and yellow with their own matching stripes.

Meg squeezes my hand. "My coat looks old and yucky."

I don't have to look at her to see how sad she is—I can hear it in her voice. I squeeze back and give our hands a little swing. What can I say? Compared to these beautiful new coats, her jacket *is* old and yucky. We walk on, and the more wonderful things we see, the more depressed we get.

"Let's play pretend, Meg." We've played the game a million and one times, but mostly with her stuffed animals lined up at a fake tea party. "We'll make up new names and pretend we're shopping, okay?"

Meg looks at me with sad eyes.

I pull her over to a bench in the center of the walkway. "I'll be Katelynn. No, there's a girl at school with that name and I don't like her. How about Angelina?" I smile at Meg, trying to draw her in. "Would you like a big sister named Angelina?"

Meg doesn't giggle or even smile. "I'd call you Angie for short."

I paste on a grin, trying to cheer her up. "So Angie for me. Now who are you?"

Meg studies the shoppers walking by with bags in their hands. "I'm Abigail."

"Angelina and Abigail." I'm not surprised Meg picked an A name to match mine, but it still makes my heart squeeze so much I hurt inside. "Do you have a nickname, sister Abigail?"

Meg gives me a weak little smile. "Abby?"

I hop off the bench and pull Meg up with me. "Let's go shopping, Abby. We need new school clothes and outfits for Thanksgiving and Christmas."

Meg is slow to get into the act. I drag her through the stores, looking at everything but new coats. We don't try anything on. Just look. I hold up a sweater and say, "Do you think this is a good color for me, Abby?"

Meg's eyes seem dull and uninterested, but I wiggle the sweater in front of my body until she tilts her head to one side and gives in to my antics. "No, Angie. It's too pinky." She pulls a red one off the rack. "Try this one. I like it better."

We keep the Angie and Abby thing going for a couple of hours while we look at jeans and t-shirts, warm sweaters and new shoes. We choose tops and long pants for Thanksgiving and party dresses for Christmas, with shoes to match. Clerks come by and ask if they can help. I smile and say, "No thanks. We're just looking." They drift away to help someone else.

"Abby," I say. "We need a Christmas present for Mom." Meg and I stand in the middle of one of the nicest stores in the mall, where mirrors and shiny, silver decorations twinkle like stars. Shoppers bustle by with bags clutched in their hands, some chattering happily with companions while others wear grim looks of determination. "What should we get her?"

Meg's little nose wrinkles in concentration. "Something pretty. Really pretty and nicer than she's ever had."

We wander through the store, passing up the ladies' clothes and shoes. All the jeans and sweaters are too practical, and Mom would have no place to wear party dresses and high heels. I hustle us by the household things like fluffy towels and gleaming china. That kind of stuff is nothing but a reminder that in real life, Mom doesn't have a home to put it in.

When we see the jewelry section, Meg and I know we've found exactly what she needs. Long glass cases full of gold and silver bracelets, earrings, and necklaces gleam under a soft glow of light. Diamonds and rubies sparkle up at us. We gaze at the treasures, hypnotized by their beauty.

A store clerk moves to the other side of the display case and asks if we need help. I glance up and smile politely. "No thanks. We're just looking."

Meg and I move to the earrings, and that's when Abby and Angie's Amazing Holiday Adventure shrivels up and dies. The clerk follows us. At first I ignore her, which is hard to do because she stands directly in front of us. I finally look up and stare right at her. She isn't smiling helpfully like clerks are supposed to look. Her fifty-something face is perfectly done without a blemish showing beneath what must be layers and layers of makeup. Cold blue eyes, behind heavy coats of shadow, liner, and mascara, glare back at me. Meg doesn't notice, chattering on about whether we should get Mom a bracelet, a necklace, or earrings.

I continue to meet the woman's frosty glare. "Why not all three?"

Meg's head pops up, and she looks at me with a wicked little grin. "Why not?" That's when Meg looks from me to the clerk and stops being Abby. The joy of our little game fades from Meg's face, tightening a rope around my heart.

"If you girls aren't buying, you need to move on." The lady cocks her head to the side and purses her lips.

I scowl at the witch, but it doesn't faze her. She wrinkles up her nose like we'll ruin the pretty things by standing too close to the display case. Meg's shoulders droop, and our game is over.

Nasty words simmer in my mouth. I ache to spew them out, to stab her over and over with their ugliness until she feels as hurt as we do, but I can't let myself say them. Not in front of Meg. Meg clutches my hand and pulls me away. We walk hand in hand through the store and out into the mall.

"Mattie?"

I whip around. Jack stands behind me, shopping bags clutched in his hands. A grin spreads across his face. "I thought that was you."

"Do you know that big boy, Mattie?" Meg whispers up at me.

"He's a friend from school." *Friend* is out of my mouth before I even think about it. I want to pull it back, erase it, and deny he means anything to me—but that would be a lie. An out-and-out lie.

Jack looks at Meg and drops to one knee. "And you must be Princess Megan."

Meg claps her hands and giggles, falling for the whole Prince Charming act. I roll my eyes and hiss at him, "No fair winning over my little sister."

Jack throws me a quirky grin but turns right back to Meg.

Meg is so excited she can't stand still. "I *am* Megan." She giggles again. "But I'm not a *real* princess. Just a *pretend* princess."

Jack shifts his packages into one hand and takes Meg by the other. "You look real to me, Princess Megan." He bows over her hand. "Sir Jackson Blake, at your service."

Meg throws me a smile so brilliant that, for one tiny second, I forget all the crummy bits of reality beating at our lives. Jack stands up, but he doesn't let go of Meg's hand. She smiles up at him with such an adoring look that I know he's won her over forever.

I scowl at him. "Seriously. You're not playing fair."

Jack laughs, shaking his head. "Not true. I told you I always wanted a little sister." He swings her hand. "How about lunch, Princess Megan? Are you as hungry as I am?"

Meg's eyes shoot over to me. "Can we, Mattie? Please?"

My throat goes dry. "We need to go to the library, Meg."

Meg's shoulders slump and her face wrinkles into a frown. "But I'm so tired of the library." She looks up at Jack. "We don't have a house anymore so we spend hours and hours and hours sitting in the library reading books."

My heart stops—quits pumping blood through my arteries and organs and all the tissue in my body. I squeeze my eyes shut and expect to collapse on the floor, dead of heart failure at sixteen.

Meg keeps right on blabbing. "Mattie made peanut butter sandwiches, but we have them all the time. And I mean *all* the time because the peanut butter and the bread won't get all rotten and stinky in the car."

I open my eyes. Jack looks straight at me. His face and body are so tense he might as well be frozen in place. Only his eyes are alive, boring deep into mine. I want to grab Meg and run, but a vision of Mom carrying Meg to Walmart slaps me in the head. I press my lips together, lift my chin, and meet his gaze straight on.

Jack's gaze doesn't waver. "Then it's settled." He keeps looking at me a long time before he glances at Meg. "Your pick, Princess."

Meg turns to me, the frown flying right off her face. "Please, Mattie? Please?"

I swallow the lump in my throat and somehow manage to nod. Meg grabs both of our hands like the three of us are one happy little family. She pulls us toward the food court, dragging us past every fast-food restaurant in the place before choosing McDonald's, like I knew she would. Jack squats by her to read the menu, and Meg picks out her Happy Meal. He stands up, turning to me.

I shake my head. "I'm not hungry."

Jack's jaw clenches, and the soft blue of his eyes turns flinty and dark.

"Mattie." He doesn't say anything else, just looks at me, long and hard. I pull my eyes away.

"Big Mac," I say.

Jack buys the whole meal deal. Fries. Drinks. Even chocolate chip cookies for dessert. We find a table and spread out our lunch. Jack asks Meg about school, and that launches her into enough chatter to fill up the entire meal. Jack sits across the table from me, his attention only leaving me long enough to ask Meg another question or to pick up a french fry.

I want to trust him. To know he won't go back to school and tell all his friends that I'm homeless, living in a car. By high school, we should be beyond all the hateful garbage kids throw at each other, but I know better. Bad things still happen to people that are poor or different or don't fit in with the rest of the crowd.

I gather up the mess from our lunch. "Time to go, Megs."

Her whole body droops. "Do we have to?"

I nod and stand up. Jack jumps to his feet, grabs the tray out of my hand, and takes it over to the garbage can. When he comes back, I stand there, gripping my backpack with both hands and wondering what happens next. Jack knows I'm homeless, knows I belong in a totally different class of people than him. Inviting us to lunch was kind and polite, but now it's over. At school, he can fade away and never speak to me again.

Meg jumps up and down. "This was the bestest lunch I ever had. Ever. Ever. Ever."

Jack leans down and takes both of Meg's hands. "I totally agree, Princess Megan."

Jack straightens up and looks at me with such a sad, sweet smile that I have to turn away. "Thanks, Jack," I say.

"That's the first time you've said my name." Jack's voice is so soft it's almost a whisper.

I sling my pack over one shoulder, grab Meg's hand, and pull her away. "We'll miss our bus."

Jack falls in beside me. "I can drive you."

"No." I keep my eyes focused straight ahead, not daring to spend another second looking into his heart-stopping blue eyes.

"I'll walk with you, then."

"No, Jack." I look straight at him. "Please. Just let us go."

Jack wrinkles up his face in a look of such worry and sadness I can barely hold my head up. "You...you can stay at our house, or...or my parents can find you a place to rent, or...or..."

I shake my head and start walking away, but he reaches over and grabs my hand. I try to pull away, but he hangs on, yanking a pen out of his pants pocket and writing a phone number across my palm.

When he finishes, he keeps holding onto my hand. "Call me if you need anything. Please?" He peers at me, his face twisted with worry. "Anything, you understand? Just tell me what you need and I'll come running."

Meg's arms hang at her side. "Goodbye, Sir Jackson Blake."

Jack lets go of my hand, squats down, and takes both of her hands in his. "Goodbye, Princess Megan. I hope to see you soon, okay?"

Meg throws her arms around his neck and gives him one of her biggest, sweetest hugs. "I like you a lot, Sir Jackson Blake."

"I like you too, Princess." Jack turns to me, taking my hand and leaning so close I'm scared he'll kiss me. "See you on Monday, Mattie?"

It's only when I nod that he lets go. As we walk away, I wonder if Jack is just being kind, or if it really doesn't matter to him that I live in a car.

CHAPTER FIFTEEN

MEG AND I STEP OFF the bus at the downtown station and walk across the street to the library. The place feels like home; I guess because it is. We settle into the teen section so I can watch *West Side Story* on the computer and Meg can curl up on the window seat with her books. I take notes on the movie and finish most of my English assignment while the afternoon drifts away.

Romeo and Juliet and *West Side Story* are so romantic, yet tragic, that I can't help but think of Jack and me. Are we star-crossed lovers, meeting at the wrong time and under the wrong circumstances? Would there be hope for us if I lived in a house in the suburbs and Mom had a stable income? Could our relationship work if we were older and wiser and had our lives all figured out?

I tell myself Jack is just a friend, but no other boy had ever made me feel so warm and comfortable. None of those other boys made my heart beat faster or my palms go all damp and sweaty when I looked at them. Jack's wide, quirky grin lights up my whole body, bringing a smile to my lips and softening my core to jelly. I shove his image into an imaginary closet in the back of my mind and slam the door. I can't go there. Not now. Not yet.

As the day wears on, my mind spins in other circles. What if the Mission is full? Can we find a room in another shelter? Before I know it, my stomach is doing backflips, and my body feels like it's dissolving into a puddle of useless skin and bone and flesh, and the inside of me—the real me—will blow apart in a million pieces.

I can't sit still. At four, I say, "Let's move to the children's section, Meg." Mom gets off work at five. She'll have to pick up Ruby at the garage, so I don't expect her before five thirty. The library closes at six—plenty of time for her to get here.

For the first hour, I don't watch the clock, but by five, I find myself constantly glancing at it. What if Mom couldn't get Ruby fixed and had to leave her in the shop? Can we get to the Mission on the bus? I know I'm being ridiculous, worrying about stuff that may never happen, but my mind churns out question after question no matter how hard I try to calm down.

Five thirty comes and goes, and I tell myself everything is fine. I check my phone. No texts. No missed calls. At a quarter to six, a man's voice fills the library: "Please exit the main doors. The library will close in fifteen minutes."

Meg's head pops up from the book she's reading, her eyes round and worried. I give her a tight smile. "Mom had to pick up Ruby at the garage." I pull her to her feet. "We'll wait by the door."

We pack away our books, go to the bathroom, and walk to the front door. After a few minutes of waiting, we follow another family outside so it isn't as obvious we're alone. I send Mom a text, telling her we're outside, but there's no response.

By six, daylight is fading, which leaves the street a charcoal gray. Streetlights flick on, filtering white light through the Oregon mist and making the sidewalks shine as if they've been polished. Passing cars whiz by, splashing water over the curb.

I check my phone to make sure I haven't missed anything. I could send another text, but what would I say? Using up phone minutes to rehash the exact same message would be a waste of money.

I guide Meg into the shadows against the library wall. We're under an overhang, but it's high above us and doesn't keep the damp and mist from soaking into my sweatshirt.

Night sinks over the street. In the glare of streetlights and cars, water droplets sparkle like diamonds against the black velvet of night. The scene reminds me of the twinkling bracelets and necklaces under the department store glass, but I can't enjoy the beauty of it. I'm too scared.

Patrons leaving the library hustle to cars or walk quickly down the street to catch the bus. Envy jabs at me. These people probably have a home, a house with a comfy chair to sit and read the books they haul away. They eat their meals at a table and sleep in a warm bed. In the mornings, they go into the bathroom to brush their teeth and take a shower, and their four walls and roof keep them warm, dry, safe, and happy. We wait and listen to the people chatter and laugh as they head out into the night.

A tall guy with dark curly hair and a black leather jacket exits the building. I can tell by his clothes he's the pushy guy from the magazine section on Thursday. Two girls—a little younger than me, but dressed way older in short skirts and tight leggings—walk beside him. I shield Meg with my body, not wanting them to see us, and we shrink deeper into the dark of our corner.

The three of them turn toward us, heading down the sidewalk, away from the library. I duck my head and hide my face in the hood of my sweatshirt. Moving could call attention to our hiding spot, so I freeze in place and hope the guy doesn't spot us. The three walk across the street. I relax and breathe, long and slow.

The last of the library users exit the building. The doors lock behind them and the lights blink out, one floor at a time. I call Mom instead of texting. No answer. The darkness deepens. We wait.

"Is Mommy okay?" Meg's voice quivers.

"She probably had a flat tire, or Ruby took a little longer to get fixed. Don't worry, Meg, everything will be okay." I say the words as if I mean them, but fear twists at me until I ache to throw my head back and scream. Everything's not all right. Mom would call or text. And even if she's fine and drives up this very instant, we're still living on the street, getting more and more bogged down by our problems.

I peer through the mist, staring at the traffic and hoping to see Ruby chugging toward us. I pull out my phone and dial the 7-Eleven. A guy answers.

"Is Rita Rollins still on duty?" I say.

"Nope," says the guy. "Left when I came in."

My stomach lurches. "How long ago was that?"

"Almost two hours, I guess."

Acid rises in the back of my throat. "Thanks." I swallow, hit the end button, and take a ragged breath to settle my nerves.

Meg clutches my hand. "Is Mommy coming?"

"She's getting Ruby fixed." I rub Meg's back. "Don't worry, Meg. She'll come."

My explanation is meant to make Meg feel better, but it sounds hollow, especially to me. Mom isn't like some parents, leaving their kids to wonder where they are or what they're doing. When Mom's late, she calls or sends a text and expects us to do the same. She gives us last-minute instructions and tells us to sit tight until she gets to us, but she never leaves us wondering. Mom takes care of us.

Something's wrong.

Meg and I sink against the wall of the library. The jerks that attacked us last night would know Ruby on sight; Mom could be on the side of a deserted road right now, fighting them off. My hands shake. I rest my lips against Meg's head and breathe in the scent of her hair.

The people that drift by terrify me. What if some psycho or grungy old drunk or spaced-out druggie comes after us? Where do we run—the bus station? It's down the street. Could we run fast enough? I keep Meg as deep into the shadows as I can.

Meg squeezes my arm. "Why doesn't Mommy call us?"

I lean over and lay my head on top of hers. "Maybe her phone is dead."

"She could borrow the garage man's."

I've always been able to make Meg feel better, to ease her worries and wash away her fears. Not this time. Anything I say would be phony, even to a kid her age. Plus, my throat is too dry to speak.

Meg doesn't complain, cry, or do what any normal six-year-old would do when they're tired, hungry, and totally scared. Instead, she presses against my side, wraps both arms around my waist, and buries her face against my soggy sweatshirt.

A car pulls up to the curb. I can't see damage to the front end, but that doesn't mean the creeps from last night aren't out looking for us. They could be using another guy's car, or this car could have a whole new creep in it, just waiting for his opportunity. I beat back my anxiety, tightening my grip to keep Meg from moving. The car idles at the edge of the street. No one gets out, no one hurries toward it. It just sits. I wait and watch. The car finally pulls away. My knees wobble, but I close my eyes and force myself to be strong.

I slide my hand into my pocket and pull out my phone. Seven forty-nine. I could send another text, but I'm worried about the minutes. Fewer and fewer people walk by. That means there aren't as many possible weirdos who could spot us, but there are also fewer people around who could help if we get attacked. We wait.

"I'm hungry." Meg mumbles the words against my sweatshirt like she doesn't want to lay another burden on my shoulders.

I slide my backpack off my shoulder. "Supper coming right up," I whisper. I unzip my pack and pull out the peanut butter sandwiches we were going to eat for lunch. I hand one to Meg and take another for myself. Meg plows right into hers. I take a bite and try to chew. The wad of dough just sits there. I force my mouth to move. Make my teeth press up and down. Push the food down my throat. I slide the rest of the sandwich back in the baggie and stuff it into my pack.

Meg hands me her empty bag. "I'm glad your boyfriend bought us lunch, Mattie."

Boyfriend? My mouth opens in protest, but I snap it shut and swallow the words. Would Jack be my boyfriend if I let him? Can I be that close to him and not end up ruining my plans for a better life? Would I end up a single parent like Mom, struggling to keep a roof over my head?

Meg wraps her arms around me and lays her head against my side. We lean against the wall and wait. I should tell her a story, one where her job is to assign names to all the characters and animals I make up—she loves that. But I can't do it; I'm too numb. Besides, our voices would draw attention from anybody wandering along the street, and I don't want to risk it.

Meg grows tired and slumps against me. Her small body gets heavier as she falls into a troubled sleep. I will my muscles and bones to stand strong and still, telling myself time goes slowly when you wait and what feels like days or even weeks is only minutes.

The reason Mom hasn't picked us up isn't because she got tired of raising two kids on her own and decided to ditch us. I know that as sure as I know the fear that grips my heart. Mom would come if she could. Sobs well up in my throat, threatening to explode into the quiet of the night. I press them deep into the pit of my gut.

If Meg and I don't have Mom, where will we go? We don't have family. Every time I ask about relatives she says we're better off alone. All those grandparents and aunts and uncles and cousins that other kids have for backup don't exist for us.

Jack gave me his phone number. I could call him, but then what? He rides in on a white horse and carries Meg and me off to his house? I've only known the guy a few days. He seems kind and thoughtful and said he would do anything to help me, but Mom has met lots of charming guys that turned out to be jerks. Jack hasn't shared where he lives or anything about his parents. I don't know if I can trust him yet.

Loud, rowdy voices mix with the buzz of cars splashing through puddles. A group of teenagers storm down the sidewalk, acting crazy and wild. Ugly words fly back and forth, like spewing out bad language is some kind of sick contest they all want to win. The group laughs at their own stupid antics and push each other around. I barely breathe. These teens are my age, but they're acting feral.

They don't move on like everyone else has. The library is dark, but they hang out by the front windows playing king of the hill on the bench near the door. The boys knock each other off, pushing and shoving. The girls pass a bottle back and forth. One of them lights up a cigarette, and the rest howl, demanding cigarettes too.

I'm terrified Meg will wake up, cry out, and give us away. Sweat breaks out on my forehead. I stand quiet and still, hoping to muffle any noise she makes against my body. Finally, the mob moves away, and the tension drains out of me, leaving my knees so weak I can barely stand.

We can't stay here. Even if we're lucky enough to stay safe from people, the cold and rain could make us sick. Especially Meg. She's too little to be out all night in her freezing wet jeans and thin little jacket.

If we go to the police station, will the cops charge Mom

with neglect? They could take us away from her, maybe split Meg and me up, and the three of us would never live together again. Meg would be alone with some strange family, and I wouldn't be there to protect her. I couldn't live with myself if something happened to my little sister when I was supposed to be taking care of her.

My feet and legs ache, and shivers run through my body. We've got to move. We've got to find a place that's warm and safe.

I slide my phone out of my pocket. Nine nineteen. I look up and down the sidewalk, but no one is around. I shake Meg's shoulder and whisper her name to wake her.

She tightens her grip around my waist and presses her face deeper into my side. "Come on, Meg." I take a step. Pain shoots down my legs. I ignore it and point down the street. "We've got to find a safer spot."

I'm so stiff I can barely walk. I check the street. A few cars drive by, but I can't see anyone on foot. I tug Meg by the hand, getting her to move. She clings to me. "You can do it." I wiggle her hand back and forth. "Stand up and walk. I know you can."

Meg's fingers dig into my sides and her face presses against me. "I'm really, really, really scared, Mattie." Her shoulders shake. "Really, really, really scared for Mommy."

"I know, Megsy." My eyes dart from the buildings surrounding us to the street to the dark shadows of an alley. "But Mom wants us to take care of ourselves, and that means you've got to stand tall and walk."

I pull her along and head toward the bus station. Two late-night riders sit on benches near their pickup points, and a few more stand or pace along the walkway. Meg and I could sit on the benches and stay dry under the shelter, but we might as well stick a neon sign over our heads that reads, "Come and get us." We'd be sitting right out in the open, and anybody walking around or driving a car could see us.

A small grocery store sits on the corner. It's closed and dark, like all the other buildings around. My instinct is to grab Meg and run to the safety of its dark walls. Instead, I force myself to keep a strong steady pace, even when we pass under the streetlight.

We get to the shadows of the store. A big metal dumpster sits back from the street, halfway down the sidewall. Hiding behind a bin of garbage grosses me out, but we move toward it anyway. The space behind the dumpster is under the eaves, so Meg and I can get out of the rain and nobody's likely to spot us. When we get close enough, I see it's a recycling bin for cardboard. No garbage. No stink.

"Mattie?" asks Meg. "Where are we going?"

"Shhhh." I glance around. No one is coming. I study the people waiting at the bus station. No one seems interested in the grocery store. I lift the lid to the dumpster and poke my head in. Cardboard. Piles and piles of flattened cardboard boxes. I prop the lid open, leaning it back against the wall.

"Come on, Meg," I whisper.

Meg whimpers. "No, Mattie."

"It's cardboard," I whisper. "Just boxes piled up."

Meg grabs me around the middle and starts to sob. "I want Mommy."

"Meg." Her name comes out too sharp, too harsh. I soften my voice. "We'll find Mommy tomorrow, but tonight we've got to stay safe and warm."

I lift Meg high enough for her to scramble into the dumpster, then I grab the edges and pull myself in. I land in a heap beside her. She's crying so loudly, I'm sure somebody will hear us.

"Shhh," I say.

I push cardboard around until I get a flat space where we can stretch out. I pull Meg up beside me and cover us both with a couple of boxes. Before I close the lid, I pull my phone out of my pocket and text Mom to let her know where we are, just in case she comes looking for us. When I'm done, I zip my phone into the front pocket of my backpack to keep it safe. Losing it in a dumpster full of boxes would be nothing short of a disaster. I reach for the lid to the dumpster, grab it, and ease it down as quietly as I can. The metal still gives off a dull clang. Meg cries out at the sound. I lie on the boxes and pull her close.

The deep black of the dumpster feels like a tomb—like Meg and I are lying in a coffin, a place you never want to go if you have the rest of your life stretching out in front of you. My eyes finally adjust. Pinpricks of gray filter in through holes and cracks in the metal. Enough light to settle my breath and calm my racing heart.

I hold Meg tight and try to relax. We're dry, and our hiding place seems safer than standing in front of the library. Mentally, I cross off my worries until a new one pops into my head—rats lurking around garbage bins. Do recycling dumpsters have mice and rats nibbling at the cardboard? Sweat beads on my forehead and trickles down the side of my face.

The dumpster is full of flattened boxes, so it's pretty clean. Nothing a rat would waste his time on with all the great garbage on the city streets. Besides, I'll take a rat before a creepy human. If a rat shows up, I'll hear it scratch and claw, and I can beat it to death with my backpack. Even a whole pack of them won't stand a chance.

The dumpster and boxes are warmer than the street. I pull another piece of flattened cardboard over us like a blanket, settle in, and close my eyes. Am I crazy for thinking I can find Mom on my own? I should give up and go to the police, but I want to keep Meg and me out of the foster system if I can. The problem with my plan is I can't know if I'm making a terrible mistake until it's too late. I close my fist over Jack's phone number, still scrawled on my hand, huddle into the boxes, and wait for morning.

CHAPTER SIXTEEN

I WAKE WITH A START. Tiny shafts of light peek through the rusty brown metal of the recycling dumpster. Tears spring to the corners of my eyes. I force them shut and fight back the sobs that rise into my throat. No Mom. No car. No home.

I concentrate on the rusted metal and take a deep breath, letting it out slow and steady. Even now, it's too dark to see how dirty the place is. It's not like whoever owns dumpsters expects people to live in them, so I can't imagine they scrub these things out, but it doesn't stink.

The gray of early dawn seeps through the holes and cracks in the metal. With one hand, I ease my phone out of the front pocket of my backpack and check the time. Seven thirteen. I stick my phone back in the pocket and zip it shut.

I lie back and close my eyes. Jack's face swims through my mind. It's silly, but just having his phone number written across my palm makes me feel less alone. I tighten my arms around Meg. We're safe. We made it through the night. Now all we have to do is find Mom.

Mom didn't call us because she can't. She must be in a coma or so hurt she can't use a phone. Shivers shoot through my body. I ignore the fear building in my head long enough to work on a plan. First, I need phone numbers for every hospital in the area, so I can call around and see if Mom was brought in as a patient. I won't let myself think about anything worse.

The creeps from the parking lot could have found her, beaten her, and done horrible things to her. My feet and hands turn numb. What if she's somewhere alone, too hurt to cry for help? I wipe away that ugly thought; instead, I picture the cops showing up, giving her first aid, and taking her to the hospital.

Meg needs sleep, but I can't lie still. "Meg." I shake her shoulder. "Wake up."

Meg groans and clutches me tighter.

"Wake up," I say. "We need to move before the grocery store opens and someone finds us."

I pry Meg's hands away, sit up, and reach for the lid to the dumpster. The top seems farther away and heavier than it did last night. I pull myself to my knees and crouch under it, pressing up. The boxes wobble and threaten to slide out from under me. The metal grinds together, but I push harder until the lid gives way and I can peek out from under it.

There's enough early morning light to give me a view of the area. I can't see anyone, but that doesn't mean much. Somebody could be standing a couple of feet away and still be out of my line of sight. I glance at the library. No one is lurking behind the building. I turn and study the alley, but no one is hanging out in that direction either. I ease up the lid of the dumpster until I can flip it back against the wall.

The metal clangs as it hits the concrete. I hold my breath and wait, but no one comes out of the store or from the back of the library. It's the best time to leave the safety of the dumpster, before the city wakes up and we're found.

Meg sits beside me cross-legged on the pile of boxes. Her face wrinkles and her lips form a rumpled line. "Where's Mommy?" Her words come out just short of a wail.

I sit back down and gather her into my arms. "We'll find her." I breathe the words into Meg's hair, kissing her head and hugging her close. "We'll find her today." Saying the words out loud gives them shape and form, strengthening my determination.

I force myself to sit still. Meg needs my hug, but all of my nerve endings seem to twitch, anxious to launch us out of the dumpster and start our hunt for Mom. I can't stay quiet for more than a few seconds before I shift my weight and the boxes slide. We've got to climb out before the store opens.

"We need to start looking, Meg. Right now." I pull away and struggle to my feet on the wobbling pile of boxes.

I grab Meg's hand, pulling her up. "You go first."

There aren't any footholds inside the dumpster. I help her climb to the edge. Her legs have to get over the rim so she can balance there until I can get her turned around. That way, I can hold her hands so she can slip down the outside of the container.

Meg starts to cry. "I'm scared, Mattie."

"I won't let you fall."

It's hard to turn Meg around to face me. Once I get her over the top, I hold tight to her hands so she can slide down the metal side. When she's almost to the ground, I let her go. She lands on her feet, and I scramble out, dropping beside her.

Meg holds up her hands, turning them back and forth so I can see them. "I'm all dirty."

I pull the sleeve of my sweatshirt down and try to scrub away the filth. "Me too, baby sister. Me too."

I close the lid of the dumpster, and we head out to the street. No rain, and luckily the pale-gray sky is clear with only a few thin clouds. It would be a perfect fall day if Mom were right here with us.

Meg wraps her arms around herself and shivers. "I'm cold."

A ripple of cold hits me too. "It's chilly, but once the sun gets higher, we'll feel better." I flip Meg's hood up and zip her jacket to the top. "We'll walk around to warm up."

Meg and I need a bathroom, but the library won't be open for hours. The bus station isn't open either, even though some buses are pulling in for their first Sunday runs. We start walking. Three blocks away from our dumpster, I spot a Porta-Potty outside a construction site.

"Look," I say. "A bathroom just for us." I paste a cheesy grin on my face, hoping my goofy attitude will cheer up my little sister.

Meg wrinkles her nose and looks at me with watery blue eyes.

"We rate it one to ten, okay? Ten is as clean as Mom can scrub a bathroom"—I stick out my tongue and cross my eyes—"and one is the dirtiest, ickiest toilet we've ever been in. Got it?"

Meg grips my hand a little tighter. "Got it."

We squeeze through a gap in the construction fence to get to the Porta-Potty. I pull open the door and gag at the smell.

Meg holds her nose with her fingers. "One?"

"Minus five," I say. "Maybe even a minus ten."

The minute we close the door, the smell slides down five more notches into the negative stink scale. I help Meg get her pants down and hold her on the seat so she doesn't have to let go of her nose. I try not to breathe, but when it's my turn, I have to gasp for a quick breath. The smell chokes me and seeps into my clothes, my hair, my skin. I hurry and pull up my jeans, wishing the hand sanitizer dispenser wasn't empty.

We break into the fresh air and slam the door behind us. At another time, one when we weren't living on the street and trying to find Mom, I might be able to laugh and giggle with Meg at how disgusting the place was. Now all I do is slip back through the fence, grateful we won't pee our pants while we wait for the library to open.

Walking the city streets tires Meg out, but it keeps us warm and feels better than waiting outside the library like we did last night. On a quiet side street, I find a bench in the sun where we can sit for a while. I dig in my pack, pull out my leftover peanut butter sandwich, and hand it to Meg.

"Do you want some, Mattie?"

Looking at the sandwich makes my stomach cramp. I tell myself the pain is from worry, but I know hunger has plenty to do with the sharp spasm tightening my gut. Yesterday's Big Mac was the last bit of food I've had, but if I remind Meg of that, she'll give up the whole sandwich without taking a bite.

"I'm not very hungry," I say, combing the tangles out of Meg's hair with my fingers. "You eat. I'll get something later." I don't tell her that we only have one dollar and twenty cents left from the money Mom gave us, which isn't enough for two bus fares, much less food.

A few cars drive by, and a couple of early morning walkers stroll along the sidewalk like it's a normal, sleepy Sunday morning. Their calmness chases away some of my fear. It's daylight. Nothing bad happened last night, and nothing bad is going to happen now.

To find Mom, I need to call the hospitals, which means getting their phone numbers. Our cell service plan is the cheapest one Mom could find, so every month we get a set amount of minutes for data, texts, and calls. I can buy more time, but I've never done it on my own.

I pull my phone out of my backpack, scroll to the icon for my service plan, and check the call minutes I have left on my cell plan. Fifty-nine minutes for calls, thirty-seven for texting, and twenty-three for data. The numbers are so low I feel queasy with worry. If I wait to look up hospital phone numbers at the library, I could use their computers to save time on data usage.

Meg nibbles on her sandwich and takes forever to finish. We're not in a hurry to get back to the library, but I get nervous a cop or a nosy person might notice us and turn us in as runaways. The fact that Meg and I don't look like sisters never worried me until Ebony said how much we stand out.

I pull the hood up on my sweatshirt, trying to hide the color of my skin, but I don't leave it up five minutes before I pull it right back off. I hate being paranoid, but Mom says hoods are scarier to some people than brown faces. Meg finally finishes the sandwich and hands over the plastic sandwich bag for me to tuck into my pack.

"The library doesn't open for a while, Meg." I stand and motion for her to follow my lead. "Let's walk around."

Meg plants her feet and won't move. "Mommy will look for us at the library."

How do I tell her Mom isn't coming? I smooth her hair and comb out a couple more tangles. "We'll go to the library, and we'll find Mom. Don't worry." My words sound flat and hollow, like deep, deep down I know I'm lying—not only to Meg, but to myself.

I take Meg's hand, and we continue walking down city blocks. We pass a church with a parking lot full of cars. People dressed in coats, dresses, and nice-looking clothes hurry toward the big double doors. Young parents carry babies and hold toddlers' hands; older people chat with clusters of friends.

Meg and I could go in, sit down, and listen to the service while we wait for the library to open. If it were raining or the weather were nasty, I wouldn't worry that our hands are dirty or that we're not wearing our best clothes. I wouldn't feel self-conscious that Meg and I are alone when other kids have at least one parent with them. I'd waltz right in holding Meg by the hand like we came every Sunday. We'd sit in a pew where it was warm and dry and listen to the music, soak in the words, and be glad for the chance to rest. But today is dry, and we have too much work to do.

Meg and I walk back toward the library. We cross the street and walk past the grocery store by the dumpster where we spent the night. The store is open now. Meg just ate, and I'm not ready to spend my last bit of cash on food, but the store might have a computer I could use to look up hospital numbers.

I push open the door.

Meg squeezes my hand. "Are we buying food?"

"No," I say, "but maybe I can get some phone numbers."

There are a couple of customers at the counter buying coffee and milk, so we have to wait our turn. The clerk is a young guy and wears a faded gray t-shirt that reads "Quack Attack" in big yellow letters. He finishes up with the person ahead of us and turns to Meg and me.

"Can I help you?"

I point at the laptop sitting on the counter. "Could you look up a couple of phone numbers for us?" I hold up my cell. "I could check, but my battery is getting low." Not true, but I'm not about to tell him I can't afford to use any more phone or data minutes.

Grinning he says, "I know how that goes." He leans on the counter with one elbow and flips open his laptop. "What do you need?"

"The hospitals."

The guy's head whips up. His eyebrows draw together and form a dark V over his nose.

"A friend had an operation yesterday," I say, "and I forgot which hospital it was." Yesterday was Saturday. Do doctors even do operations on Saturdays? The excuse is so lame I know he doesn't buy it. I try to think of something smart to add, words that would make my story sound halfway real, but my mind is nothing but an empty, black pit. All I can do is give the guy a weak smile and hope he helps us.

The clerk types in the words and studies the screen. I can see Meg out of the corner of my eye, but I don't dare look at her, or I'll lose my nerve. I use the time to dig a pen and a scrap of notebook paper out of my pack. The clerk reads off the numbers for two hospitals, and I write them down.

"Thanks." I hold up the paper I've written on. "Thanks a lot."

His eyes take on that quiet, sad look that people get when they know you're not telling them the truth. "Anything else I can do?"

I shake my head. "No. But thanks again."

My knees are so weak I can hardly make my legs work. What do I expect him to do? Call the cops? The guy probably will forget us the minute we're gone. I keep right on walking out the door and don't breathe until I'm standing on the sidewalk.

"You lied to that nice man, Mattie."

Meg spits the words out so they aren't just a statement of fact, but an accusation. I take a quick breath and bite my lower lip. "Yes, I did."

Meg's blue eyes shoot darts through me. "Mommy said we're supposed to tell the truth every time. Every single time."

An intense sense of grief and sadness washes over me, making it hard to breathe. Mom is gone, and I miss her so much every muscle and cell in my body hurts.

"Mom's right, Meg. We've got to be honest. Especially to each other." I plant a kiss on the top of her head. "But sometimes we have to do things that don't seem right, even though we don't want to."

My words sound lame, like people can wash away guilt by tacking on that flimsy phrase. As if there is no real right or wrong in the world, just all this gray fuzz in the middle that never allows for a straight path.

I swallow the grief welling in my throat. "If I tell everyone the truth, Meg, we could get taken away from Mom and put into foster care."

The anger on Meg's face mixes with these new worries and builds up in her eyes. It's too hard for me to keep looking at her, so I grab her hand and we walk up the block to the front of the library. I'm anxious to call the hospitals, but I take the time to settle Meg on the bench out front so I can concentrate on making the calls. Meg swings her legs back and forth while I pull a book out of her backpack. She looks at the book but doesn't reach out and take it. I lay the book on the bench beside her and pull out my phone.

The clerk gave me two numbers. I start with the first. A receptionist answers, "McKenzie-Willamette Medical Center."

"Could you tell me if a Rita Rollins was admitted last night?" The words fly out of my mouth in a rapid stream.

Meg's face wrinkles and her eyes zero in on me. I try to smile at her while I wait for the answer, but forcing a cheery attitude is too hard. I turn away and study the cars passing by on the street.

Even if Mom couldn't tell the doctors who she was, wouldn't someone look through her backpack and find her wallet and phone? That scenario only works if Mom had her pack with her. Those scumbags from the parking lot could have taken it to cover up the crime.

The receptionist comes back on the line. "No. We don't have anyone listed by that name."

"Did a woman come in without a name?" I say. "She's thin and not very tall and white with long, light blondish-brown hair, and she's only thirty-three." I take a breath to slow myself down. "Did anyone like that come in?"

The receptionist hesitates. "I'm sorry. There were no unidentified patients admitted either."

"Okay," I say. "Thanks."

I end the call and punch in the number for RiverBend Hospital. A recorded message in three languages instructs me to press one or stay on the line if I speak English. The same voice says all the operators are busy, and my call will be answered in the order it was received. I wait, picturing the seconds adding up to minutes of call time clicking off my phone.

Meg grabs the sleeve of my sweatshirt and tugs it back and forth. "Is Mommy sick?"

I keep my phone pressed against my ear and slide my other arm around Meg's shoulders. Why didn't I tell her what I was doing? Did I think she couldn't handle the thought of Mom being too sick or hurt to get to us? Meg spent the night in a recycling dumpster. She can handle the truth.

"Is that why you're calling the hospitals, Mattie?"

"I thought Mom got in an accident and couldn't call us," I say.

Meg studies me with serious eyes that seem too old for a six-year-old. "But she didn't?"

"She's not at the first hospital," I say. "We'll see about the second one."

The recording repeats, "Thank you for your patience. All of our operators are busy. Please stay on the line and your call will be answered in the order it was received."

More minutes tick off my phone. What if I run out of cell time and Mom isn't able to call me? When we got short on minutes before, Mom would buy enough extra to get us to the end of the month, but I don't know how she did it. Plus, it takes money I don't have.

I'm startled when an operator says, "RiverBend. How may I help you?"

Precious seconds tick by before I think of what to say. I drop my arm from Meg's shoulder and clutch my phone to my ear. "Do you have a Rita Rollins as a patient?

"Let me connect you with the front desk," the woman says.

Meg scrambles to her knees so she can lean her head close to mine and hear what's being said. "RiverBend. How may I help you?"

I repeat my request, but there's no Rita Rollins checked in. "What about somebody that doesn't have an ID on them and isn't awake enough to give their name? Like a Jane Doe person."

"That would be an unidentified trauma patient," says the receptionist. "I'll check to see if we have anyone like that, but there is no way to know if the patient is Rita Rollins."

The word trauma makes my mind spin through pictures of bloody gunshot wounds, grizzly car accidents, and horrific beatings. Just hearing the receptionist say the word scares me so much I can hardly reply to thank her.

The woman comes back and says, "We do have an unidentified person checked into the ER."

My hand shakes. "A woman that's not very tall and has light blondish-brown hair and blue eyes and some week-old bruises on her face?"

"I'm sorry," says the receptionist. "I don't have that information, but I can call down there and see if the patient is a man or a woman."

The tremors in my hand move through my entire body making it hard to hold my phone. "Thanks." I glance over at

Meg. Her mouth puckers and twists back and forth like she wants to cry but won't let the tears run.

The receptionist takes several minutes to get back to me. "The patient *is* a young woman," she says.

I don't know whether to be happy that the woman lying in the emergency room might be Mom or terrified because she's hurt so bad she can't tell the doctors who she is.

Somehow I manage to blurt out, "Thanks. How do we find out if this person is…" I almost say *our mom*, but catch the words before they spill out of my mouth. "Rita Rollins?"

"You will have to come down to the hospital to identify her."

"Thanks," I say. "We will. We'll come right now."

I end the call and turn to Meg. We stare at each other, our eyes wide and only inches apart. "Is it Mommy?" Meg whispers so softly I barely hear her.

Hope and fear battle inside my head. I want this unidentified person to be Mom, *need* her to be Mom, so Meg and I can stop worrying. But thinking of Mom so badly hurt she can't talk or think terrifies me. "It could be. We'll just have to go and see."

A dollar and twenty cents is all the money I have for bus fare. I turn away from Meg, dig my wallet out of my pack, and count out the money. "We've got bus money for me, but you'll have to pretend you're five." I raise my eyebrows and twist my mouth to the side. "There is no other way to get there. Besides, the bus driver probably won't ask your age."

Meg sets her lips in a straight little line and nods her head. "Mommy will say it's okay to be five for a while."

"You're right, Meg. Mom would understand." I grab her hand. "Let's go."

CHAPTER SEVENTEEN

THE MAP AT THE BUS station shows the fastest route is an EmX bus to the Springfield station and then to RiverBend. Meg and I walk to the right stop and stand in the warmth of morning sun, waiting until an extralong green bus pulls up and we can get on.

The EmX speeds along, pulling in and out of designated stops. My eyes take in the buildings, trees, traffic, and people around me, but the images flow into a blur of color and don't register with my brain. Instead, I sit in my seat, rigid with both hope and anguish, while my thoughts whirl.

One minute, I imagine Meg and me running into the hospital, finding Mom, and throwing our arms around her. The three of us will laugh and squeal and disrupt the whole building. Even if Mom is too hurt to be awake, Meg and I will hurry to her side, hold her hand, and snuggle close. Life will be whole and good again.

Then fear wins the war in my brain, and I am overcome with dread. What if Mom dies before we get to the hospital? What if Meg and I have to identify her body instead of run into her arms? My stomach contracts and threatens to throw up its contents, even though there's nothing there but acid. I pull tiny bits of air into my lungs until the pain eases enough for me to breathe again.

We stop at the Springfield station, but I am too fearful to focus on anything but losing Mom. To stay sane, I pull out my phone and force myself to concentrate. I scroll through the icons, clicking on the one for our service provider and seeing that the calls to the hospital cost me twenty-eight minutes. Bile rises into my throat. Can I add time without Mom's credit card? There is no way to know unless I go through the process.

Every tap on the screen feels like bags of cement are taped to my arms. Will Mom be alive? Will she recognize us? I read the prompts, but it feels like centuries for the words to travel from my eyes along jumbled nerve endings and finally connect to my brain.

At no time does the program ask me to pull the last few cents out of my pocket or give them the number of Mom's credit card to pay for the minutes. I click on twenty dollars of time to be added to our account and nearly cry. Mom has to work that much longer and harder to get us an apartment.

My phone lies in my hand while I stare at the number of minutes left on my cell, but the number doesn't automatically change. How long does it take before my twenty dollars' worth of time is added? Fifteen minutes? An hour? Three days? I force myself to look away.

The EmX bus pulls to a stop in front of RiverBend Hospital. The building is beautiful; made of red brick, it stands several stories tall and stretches out for what looks like a couple of city blocks. The hospital is set in front of a backdrop of dark-green trees and the landscaping out front is designed with shrubs and grasses that look good even in November.

Meg and I step off the bus and walk toward a large covered entrance. Mom has driven us by RiverBend several times, but we have never been inside. The reception area is so spacious and elegantly furnished we both stop to stare.

"Wow," says Meg. "This place is really pretty."

Wood railings and paneling, comfy chairs and tables, and lots of natural light give the entrance the look of a first-class hotel. Long hallways stretch out on both sides of the main doors, and a gift shop sits off to the side, though the glass doors are closed for business this early on a Sunday morning. In front of us stands a desk in warm wood tones with a sign saying "Information." Meg and I hold hands and walk over to the receptionist.

The woman behind the desk looks up and says, "Hi, how may I help you?" She is an older person, with silver hair dropping to her shoulders and a spray of tiny lines fanning out from the corners of her eyes.

"I called earlier and was told there was an unidentified woman as a patient in the emergency room?" I push back the fear piling in my throat. "We came to identify her."

The receptionist points down the hallway to our right. "Head down to ER. They'll tell you what to do." The woman's forehead scrunches up, making the lines around her eyes deeper. "But isn't there an adult with you? Someone else who can identify the woman?"

I blurt out my story as rapidly as I can. "Our dad's parking the car. He'll be here in a minute." I don't give her a chance to ask us any more questions. "Thanks."

When we get far enough away from the information desk so the receptionist can't hear, I lean over and whisper, "I'm sorry, Meg. I hate all these stories as much as you do, but I don't know what else to do."

Meg looks at me, her face tight with worry. "I know, Mattie. You said we've got to make up stuff."

At the emergency room, three people stand in line at the check-in desk. A man dressed in dirty jeans and an even dirtier t-shirt clutches a bloody rag over a gash on his hand, and a young woman cradles a crying infant in her arms. The third person is an old man pushing a woman in a wheelchair. The woman sags in the seat, her stringy white hair draping over her face. The ER isn't crowded, and the two women behind the desk are quick and efficient, but it still seems like an eternity before it's our turn.

"We're here to identify the woman that came in earlier and didn't have a name." I point down the hallway toward the main entrance. "The receptionist down there said you had a patient that hadn't been identified and we could come and see if she is Rita Rollins."

The young woman looks around. "You have an adult with you? A parent?"

"Dad is at work and will lose his job if he leaves. We're here to see if your patient is our mom."

I pull Meg a little closer and point out what is so obvious to me. "We're sisters, and Dad will come as soon as he can."

The woman studies us, then picks up a phone. "I don't know the exact status of that patient, but give me your name, and I'll send a nurse out to talk to you."

"Mattie and Meg Rollins."

The woman points to the chairs in the waiting room. "Have a seat. The nurse will call you."

Meg and I drift over to a pair of chairs sitting close to the front desk. Meg scoots into the seat and shifts her backpack onto her lap. I do the same. Our bodies are stiff with worry. Is Mom lying in a hospital bed just beyond those closed doors? Are we close enough to yell and she would hear us? Or is she hurt so bad that she won't even know we found her?

Names are called for other patients, but we wait. More people enter the ER through the wide glass doors and are checked in by the women at the desk. Finally, a male nurse in blue scrubs steps out and calls, "Mattie and Meg Rollins?" We jump to our feet and hurry across the room.

The nurse is Darren's size with short brown hair and serious brown eyes. His body holds a tension that doesn't ease when we step up to him.

"The patient you asked about has already been identified and is on the way to surgery." His words come at us in such a rapid stream they don't sink into my head before he turns to leave.

I grab at his bare arm. "Wait. Wait a minute. What do you mean the woman was identified?"

The nurse looks annoyed and pulls his arm away. "The woman's parents came in an hour ago, gave us her name, and signed all the papers for surgery." He turns and walks back through the doors to the ER before we can waste any more of his time.

Meg and I stand rooted to the floor, our hopes crushed. My grand plans for a happy reunion—the visions of finding Mom and taking care of her—vanish and leave my mind dark and empty. Meg squeezes my hand and whispers, "If Mommy isn't here, then where is she?"

"I don't know, Meg." My words taste sour. "I don't know."

We walk back to the main lobby, but I have no more sense of direction than if I were walking in a dense fog or a blinding snowstorm. My actions are automatic, my muscles having walked this way only a short time before. Meg turns us toward the front entrance, but something holds me back.

"Wait, Meg," I say. "Let me think a minute." I pull her over to a couch and sink into it.

Meg stands in front of me. "We need to get on that big green bus and go back to the library because that's where Mommy will look for us, and we need to go right now."

"We'll go, Meg," I say. "Let me have a couple of minutes, okay?"

Meg sighs, raising her shoulders up and down in a dramatic gesture. She drops onto the couch beside me and perches on the front edge. I stare at the lobby with blank eyes and try to think.

Mom isn't lying here in a coma, so where is she? If she wasn't admitted to the hospital for treatment from a car accident or for any other horrid reason, does that mean she was dead at the scene? Thinking about where police take bodies revs my heart rate so high my brain locks up, refusing to function.

Meg squirms beside me, sighs again, and finally says, "Please, Mattie? Can't we go? Please?"

I pat her on the back, but the rest of my body stays still and rigid. Should I call the police and ask them if there was a bad accident last night? Or can I call directly to the city morgue? Could the receptionist at the information desk make the calls for me? She would know who to call and probably get more answers than if I tried to call on my own. Plus, using her phone would save precious airtime on mine.

"I've got an idea, Meg." I stand, and Meg pops up beside me.

"We're going back to the library?"

"Not yet," I say. "First, I've got to ask the lady at the desk more questions, and maybe she can make some phone calls for us."

I turn toward the desk, but freeze. The receptionist is watching us. There are several other people in the area, but the woman is zeroed in on Meg and me. I told the woman our dad was parking the car, so if I go back to her now, she'll be suspicious of me.

I put my arm around Meg's shoulders and steer her back down the hallway to the ER. Meg pulls away and crosses her arms. "Where are we going?"

Her face is set in a deep frown, and her voice is so loud it rattles through the hallway. "Why aren't we getting on the bus?"

I lean down and whisper. "Shhh. Don't look, but the lady at the desk is watching us, so we can't go back and talk to her."

Meg spins her head around so she can see the receptionist, even though I just told her not to. I sigh and glance over to see the woman still intent on every move we make.

"See?" I rest my hand on her shoulder and give it a gentle squeeze. "We need to go back to the emergency room for just a little while." My squeeze turns into a pat. "I know the waiting is hard, Meg, but hang on a little longer, okay?"

Meg lets her arms drop to her sides, but her face doesn't let go of its pouty frown. We walk back to the ER and get in line. There are more people ahead of us this time, so it takes longer to get to the receptionist.

When we finally step in front of her, the woman gives us a questioning look. "Hi again. Was the woman your mother?"

"No," I say. "That person was already identified by somebody else, but now we're really scared Mom died in a car accident and was taken directly to the city morgue." I don't have to fake the terror eating away at my self-control. "How do we check?"

Meg hears me say the word "died" and tightens her grip on my hand so much my fingers hurt from the pressure.

The woman leans across the desk. "The city morgue is housed in this building, but you girls need to call an adult. If your mom *was* killed last night, you need to have a family member or an adult friend with you."

"Meg and I just need to know if there is a *possibility* that Mom is there, and if there is, Dad will leave work."

The receptionist studies us for a long time before she reaches for her phone. She taps in a number and says, "Hi. This is ER. Do you have an unidentified woman that has expired in the last twenty-four hours?"

I say, "Ask for a Rita Rollins too, just in case she had her name with her, but no contact information."

The woman adds, "And can you check for a young woman by the name of Rita Rollins as well?"

The receptionist listens to the answer and hangs up her phone. "No Rita Rollins and no unidentified woman." The woman's face is kind, but lined with worry. "Why don't you girls stay here until your dad comes? His boss will understand this is an emergency."

I nod, as relief rushes through me. Mom isn't dead, lying on a cold slab in the bowels of the building. "Thanks for your help. I'll call Dad right now." I pull my phone out of my pack, tap the screen, and put it to my ear.

I turn to go, pretending I'm talking to my dad on the phone, instead of wondering where to go and what to do next.

CHAPTER EIGHTEEN

I SHOULD BE HAPPY. GIDDY, EVEN. Mom is not in a drawer at the city morgue or unconscious in the hospital. But all I feel is empty.

Meg and I walk out of the building through the emergency room entrance. We step through the doors, but instead of heading straight for the bus stop, I pull Meg over to a bench where we are out of sight of the reception areas. I slide onto it, feeling as old and sick as the woman in the wheelchair. For no reason I can think of, I'm not ready to leave the hospital.

All my ideas of people to call or places to go are gone. Mom is out there somewhere, but I'm no closer to finding her. Am I overlooking something important—some clue that should be obvious, but I'm too tired and scared to find it?

Meg pokes me in the arm. "Aren't we going to the library, Mattie?"

When I don't respond right away, she pokes me over and over again until I know I've got a whopper of a bruise blossoming on my side.

"Mommy won't find us here." Meg steps in front of me, gripping the backpack on her shoulders with both hands. "She'll go to the library, and when we're not there, she'll get scared and won't know what to do."

I pull myself to my feet. Why not go back to the library? Meg will be happy, and that will give me time to think. "We should go to the bathroom and get a drink before we start back."

Meg grabs my hand and pulls me toward the bus stop. "I can wait till the library and so can you."

Meg drags me across the street. I sink onto the bench by the bus stop, but Meg stands and watches the road. She wiggles her knees back and forth, willing our ride to hurry. In a couple of minutes, the EmX bus drives up, and Meg pulls me toward the door. I dig the transfer ticket out of my jeans pocket, grateful I remembered to ask for one when we arrived.

My actions have no more life than a robot or a machine programmed to walk and talk but not to think. Meg is the opposite, brimming with energy. She wiggles and squirms on the bus seat while she stares out the side window. We pass through the Springfield station and continue on to Eugene.

Meg explodes off the seat as soon as the bus gets close enough for her to see the library. She grabs my hand and drags us to the front so we can hop out the minute the doors open. Meg and I step onto the sidewalk and start for the building.

"Mom isn't waiting for us, Meg." Telling her that we're alone makes me want to throw up. "She would text or call if she could, so that means she can't get to us."

Meg keeps dragging me along until we cross the street and are right in front of the library. "I *know* that, Mattie, but when she *can* look for us, this is where she'll come."

We enter the building and head straight for the bathrooms and drinking fountain. I drink a ton of water and hope that filling up my stomach will make me feel less hungry. It doesn't work.

I help Meg pick out new books and spread her things out on the little table where that cute monster of a boy nearly got us kicked out. I am numb to it all.

When Meg is settled, I drop onto the couch and watch my baby sister read through her stack of books. She's calm and content. All the early morning anxiety is gone, and she's back to her sweet little self. To Meg, the library has turned into our house, a place she feels safe and protected; as long as I'm with her, she could stay forever.

I sit on the couch and stare off into space. There must be places I could look, things I could do, or clues I've missed that would lead me to Mom. Bits and pieces of our lives flit through my mind, but nothing gels into an idea or a plan.

I glance over at the clock and realize almost an hour has gone by. I blink at the numbers, thinking I'm not reading it right. I never just veg out like some spaced-out pothead. People in class do it all the time, but not me. I pay attention and soak up every little scrap of knowledge the teachers throw out to me.

My brain is fuzzy, full of empty air and meaningless thoughts that don't connect. It doesn't feel like my mind at all. I grab my backpack and pull out a notebook and pencil. Maybe if I write everything down, I'll be able to concentrate enough to make sense of it all. I open my notebook and stare at the blank paper. It takes me forever to write the word *hospital*. I cross it out and write *car accident*. I start to draw a line through that too, but stop halfway across the word.

The police. Should I contact them? Mom isn't in the hospital or the city morgue. She could still have been in a car accident, but if the accident wasn't bad enough to go to the hospital, she would've called us. I finish scratching *car accident* off my list. If I can't find Mom by myself, I'll call the cops, but right now, they'll ask questions I don't want to answer.

My pencil rests against the paper while seconds tick off the clock. I finally add *freaks from Friday night* to my list and put a giant question mark beside the words. I'm tempted to cross them out, but what if Mom got nabbed *before* she picked Ruby up at the garage? What if they didn't run her off the road or smash up the car, but kidnapped her?

The idea makes sense, except the parking lot guys wouldn't recognize Mom without Ruby. It was too dark and our windows were all fogged. But they could have run Mom off the road and kidnapped her when she crashed Ruby. For that matter, anyone could have done the same thing. To find out if Ruby was in a car wreck, I'm back to talking to the police.

I write down *kidnapped* and put a question mark by it, but the idea that Mom wasn't with Ruby hangs with me. If I knew the name of the garage where Mom went for repairs, I could call them to see if she picked up the car. The problem is that it's Sunday, and no one would be working. Bits of thoughts flit back and forth through my head, prickling my senses. I should be close to the answer, but I'm too slow and groggy to think of it.

My stomach cramps. Yesterday's Big Mac was a year ago. That's probably why my brain is functioning so slow I might as well be in a coma. Thinking about food makes my stomach knot up even more. I root around in the bottom of my backpack for any scrap of food I can find but only come up with bent paper clips and scraggly hair bands.

Meg sets her book on the little table. "I've got to go potty."

"We need to move anyway." I stuff my notebook in my backpack, zip it shut, and push myself to my feet. The room spins. I grab the couch arm and take a deep breath. Food. I need to eat, but we've only got a few cents left from the money Mom gave us. I've still got a key to Darren's apartment. I should stake out his place, wait until he leaves, and raid his refrigerator.

Energy surges through my veins. Darren. My head pops up. My hands clench. He knows Mom works at the 7-Eleven, so he could have waited outside and nabbed her when she got off work. Would he kidnap Mom? Commit an actual crime like that? He hit her—I never thought he'd do that, and Mom didn't either, or she wouldn't have stuck with him for two and a half years.

"Mattie?"

I glance at Meg. She has her backpack on and is looking at me with her eyebrows pulled together and her nose all squished up.

"Are you okay?"

I'm too busy thinking of Darren to focus on my sister. "Yeah. I'm okay." I take her hand and give it a squeeze. "Let's go to the bathroom."

To find Mom, we've got to go back to Darren's apartment, and the few cents I have in my pocket aren't enough. Somehow, I've got to earn some money. We finish up in the bathroom and get another drink. I steer Meg out the front door.

"Can't we stay in the library, Mattie?"

"I've got an idea." I stand on the sidewalk and look down the street toward the corner grocery. I could ask the clerk if he needs someone to do chores, like sweeping and stocking shelves. That would be honest work, but the sales clerk already suspects Meg and I are homeless or on the run. Asking for a job might push him right into calling the cops.

Stealing somebody's purse or wallet is out of the question. It's totally wrong; plus, I'd get caught, end up in jail, and Meg would be put in foster care anyway. That leaves begging for money. Asking people on the street if they'll give me the change in their pockets. Street kids panhandle all the time, so I've got to swallow my pride and try it.

People drift by, and I decide I can't have Meg with me. Even if she helps reel in people with big, soft hearts, it wouldn't be right to use her like that. I glance over at the bench. Meg could sit where she'd be right in front of me, and I could keep a close eye on her—but I'd feel like such a lowlife, corrupting my sweet sister with the scuzzy need to beg. I look at the kiosk by the front door. The coffee shop is all windows, floor to ceiling. Meg could sit at one of the little tables reading her books, so I could see her and she could see me.

"Come on." I lead her back through the door and over to a table. "You're going to sit here where it's warm and watch me, and I'm going to be out there on the sidewalk."

Meg's eyes get big and round, and she shakes her head back and forth so fast her hair flies. "No, Mattie, no."

I ignore the fear stamped all over her face, pull out a chair, and help her slide out of her backpack. I sit her down and squat beside her. "Look." I point outside. "You'll be able to see me every minute, and I can see you." I pull a book out of her pack and lay it on the table in front of her. "We need bus fare, and that means I have to ask people for the money." I run my hand over her head and smooth her hair. "Mommy may be at Darren's, and we don't have enough money to get there."

"Can't we call Mommy?"

"She's not answering, sweetie." I pick up Meg's hand and kiss it. "We've got to go to Darren's place and get her." I lay her hand back in her lap and study her sweet little face. "If anyone comes near you, bang on the glass and scream. Okay?"

Meg nods. Leaving her terrifies me, but I stand and walk out the door, never taking my eyes from her. As I get out to the sidewalk, I keep glancing back through the windows, checking to make sure she's safe. I position myself so I'm directly across from her with my back to the street. Meg stares out at me with big eyes. I wave, and she waves back.

I turn my attention to the people walking by. How do I choose? Women? Men? Young people? Old people? I pick out an older woman. "Ma'am?" I say, but she's already past me and heading into the library.

Lesson one: talk fast. A young man with baggy jeans and long greasy hair saunters by. I let him go. He doesn't look like he has any more money than I do. I spot a middle-aged man in a suit. "Sir?" I shove out my hand and talk as fast as I can. "Could you spare a—"

The man curls his lip and sneers, "Get a job, you lazy punk."

I yank back my hand and grit my teeth. The guy is a first-class moron, but his comment still stings. I glance over at Meg. She sees me looking at her and waves both hands in that fluttery little-girl way she has. I take a deep breath, blow it out in a rush, and get back to work.

The next person I try is a young woman, but she totally ignores me. I try not to think, just stick my hand out and ask anyone who walks by if they could spare some change. My pitch gets faster, but it doesn't seem to help.

"You're pitiful."

I swing around, expecting the put-down to come from some well-dressed lady with a designer purse stuffed full of cash. It's Ebony. Her spiky black hair sticks out around the same gray hoodie she had on the night I met her. Ripped jeans, too faded and baggy to be in style, hang loose on her thin frame. Black boots with heavy soles cover her feet.

Ebony shakes her head and rolls her eyes. "You really don't have a clue, do you?"

I stick my chin in the air. "I'm managing."

"How much money have you raked in?"

When I don't answer, Ebony laughs. "Thought so." She glances around. "Where's your little sister?"

I nod toward the coffee shop. "Watching me through the window."

Ebony gives me a sideways smile. "Smart. Using her could bring the cops."

That's not the reason I set Meg in the coffee shop, but I don't tell Ebony that.

Ebony's face turns serious. "You're standing too far away. You've got to be close enough so people can't ignore you, but not so close you make them nervous." Ebony points to a place on the sidewalk closer to the front door. "Stand over there. People will have to walk right by you to get into the library."

She turns back to me. "And give them a sob story. Don't just ask for change. They think you're buying drugs. Even if you are, give them a reason to feel good."

Ebony points her thumb over her shoulder. "I'll stand back and give you pointers."

"Wait. I'm not ready." The words fly out of my mouth sounding weak and whiny, even to me.

Ebony rolls her eyes, steps back, and leans on a parking meter.

Meg's still sitting right by the window, watching me. I wave and turn my attention back to my job. I need a sad story. One that will pull at people's hearts but that I can spit out in a hurry. The truth is way too complicated.

People keep passing. I take a deep breath to work up my courage and step closer to the front door of the library. People have to pass close by me, but I'm not blocking their way. A young guy in a University of Oregon sweatshirt heads across the sidewalk. I pick him out as my best chance, and the minute he gets close, I spew out my story as fast as I can.

"Bus fare to get home?" The guy doesn't look at me, but he hesitates enough for me to blurt out, "Please, mister. I'm trying real hard to get off the street. I just need a little more money, and I can go home."

It works. The guy comes to a stop, pulls his wallet out of his jeans, and hands me a dollar. I'm so overcome with the money in my hand, I can hardly stammer, "Thanks. Thanks a lot."

Confidence. That's what surges through me. I try everyone. Old people. Young people. Rich. Poor. In a way, my story is true. I *am* trying to get home, and I *am* trying to get off the street. Most people don't stop, but enough of them dig into their pockets that I make bus fare and am on my way to buying Meg and me some food.

I am so focused on panhandling that a police officer is only a couple of steps away before I spot him. His body is tall and blocky, giving him a sense of authority and control. The navy blue of his uniform stretches tight over the vest he wears, and his face is lined with a scowl that makes me drop my hand and hold my breath to keep from crying.

"What do you think you're doing?" He clips every word off at the end like he wants to make certain I don't miss a single one.

The weak, insecure part of me wants to give up and confess Meg and I are homeless and Mom is missing. The police have resources and experience to help find her, but Meg and I could land in foster care—who knows if Mom would ever get us back.

My mind spins so fast I can't decide what to do. Am I making a mistake by not telling the police Mom is missing? I won't endanger Meg for another night, that is certain, but I also want to find Mom myself and keep us together if I can.

I force myself to be brave and look the policeman right in the eye. "Is it illegal to panhandle? I see people doing it all the time."

The cop twists up his mouth. "Look, miss. Whether panhandling is legal or not is irrelevant." He puts his hand over his mouth and slides it down his face until it drops to his side. "I hate to be blunt, but you are a target for every pimp in Eugene. You're African-American, so you stand out in this lily-white town of ours. Plus, you're young and I'm guessing homeless or a runaway. Those guys hunt for kids like you. They prey on teens, but especially girls."

My legs turn to water and my knees grow so weak they threaten to collapse. Was the guy wearing that black leather jacket a pimp? He walked by Friday night with two girls that looked younger than me. Does he lure kids into hanging with him and then feed them into a system of prostitution and human trafficking? He didn't say or do anything wrong, but he still scared me. I stiffen my legs into posts and stand strong, but I can't keep the tears from springing to my eyes.

The officer throws his arm out toward a group of kids hanging out on the corner across the street. "I know those kids. Most of them have been on the street a while."

He turned back to me. "But I spotted you a block away because you're new. That means pimps and traffickers and half the bottom-feeders in Eugene are watching you too."

The policeman's broad shoulders rise and fall with a hopeless sigh. "Homeless people and runaways get beat up, raped, robbed, and even killed. And half the time, no one knows or even cares."

He glances back in time to see tears slide down the side of my face. "You are in real danger, miss. Go home, go to a friend's house, or find a shelter." His serious brown eyes search my face. "But get off the street. Understand?"

I nod and watch the officer walk toward the black-and-white squad car parked in the drop-off zone. My body feels hollow, empty of bones or muscles or enough organs to sustain life. I need food, but my weakness is not just from a few missing calories.

Meg. I quickly turn back to see her nose and hands pressed against the glass of the kiosk. I paste a limp smile on my face and wave. She waves back.

Ebony walks up beside me. "You okay?"

I sigh. "Yeah."

"What did the cop want?"

I look over at her. "He told me the same things you did. I stand out because of my brown skin, and that I'd better get off the street." I stick my hand in my pocket. Most of the money is small coins, but I pull out the dollar bill the first guy gave me. "Here."

"Don't be a dork." Ebony waves the money away. "I don't need it."

I should fight her over it, but somehow all that comes out is, "Thanks."

Ebony looks straight into my eyes. "The cop is right, Mattie. Get off the street."

My chin pops up. "You're making it."

Ebony shakes her head and makes a little snort with her mouth. "I live in a house in the suburbs with a mom and dad and a dog named Ralph."

My mouth drops open. "You're not a runaway?"

"No, but don't spread that around." She waves her hand at the library. "The kids in there think I am."

"Then why aren't you at home?" Constantly hanging out at the library when you don't have to is so foreign that I can't even process the idea. "Why aren't you curled up with your dog watching TV, or eating pancakes with your parents, or just sitting in your room with a pile of books?"

Ebony shrugs her thin shoulders. "Got sick of my life, I guess." She glances over at the coffee shop. Meg stares out the window and gives us another cute two-handed wave.

Ebony waves back at her. "A few years ago, Mom and Dad kind of gave up on the whole parenting thing, so I gave up on their happy-little-family thing."

We stand side by side. Not talking. Just thinking. For me, I realize how lucky I am. No matter how tough our life gets, Mom devotes herself to her kids. She pours all her love into us and gives us every scrap of energy she has.

Meg keeps staring out the window at me, never moving an inch. "I've got to go." I turn to Ebony. "Thanks again." I pat the pocket of my jeans, bulging with change. "This is enough for now, and hopefully I never need to beg for cash again."

Ebony's eyes soften, making her black eyeliner stand out as too harsh for the sweetness of her face. "Good luck."

CHAPTER NINETEEN

GOING BACK TO DARREN'S APARTMENT makes my skin turn cold and prickly. The guy's a low-life jerk for getting drunk and taking out his frustration and anger on Mom. But would he really kidnap her? Snatching somebody could land him in jail for years, but I suppose a scumbag like Darren could do just about anything if he got tanked up enough.

Meg and I stand at the bus stop and hold hands. I stare down the street—like I can't wait for the bus to get here—but it's all a mask. I keep myself as calm and quiet as I can on the outside, but inside I'm a wreck. Worries, questions, and fears swirl through every cell in my body.

Could Darren even pull off a kidnapping? Wouldn't Mom fight him with every breath she had? How would he get her into his truck if she was kicking and screaming? A new thought hits me. What if he didn't take her to his place, and I never find her? I press my lips together and swallow the nausea that surges up my throat and into my mouth.

A bus pulls up at the stop behind us. People get off, and others line up to get on. I turn and watch, not because I care, but because I don't dare let myself think through all the horrible possibilities battering me. The bus driver steps off and stretches. She paces around the sidewalk for a minute or two before she climbs back on and drops into the driver's seat. A couple of kids hurry to the bus door. Just before they step on, one of them drops a half-eaten Whopper into the trash.

My body reacts before my brain has time to think. I jump toward the garbage can and snatch the sandwich off a heap of crumpled plastic bags. Before I can get it to my mouth and take a bite, a man's dirty hand clamps onto my wrist. I stare up at a scraggly guy, not much older than me. His dirty blond hair is short and choppy, sticking up in tufts all over his head. His eyes are dark and wild. I tighten my grip on the Whopper, narrowing my eyes. "Back off."

Meg grabs my other arm with both her hands and tries to tug me away. "Mattie! No!"

I ignore her and stare at the guy holding my arm. "Let go, or I'll scream my head off."

The guy leans toward me and crushes my wrist. His body odor is so strong that my nose wrinkles and my stomach churns.

"No you won't." That's all he says, but his eyes say the rest. He'll break my arm before he lets go. I grit my teeth and hang on, hoping I'll be wise enough to drop the burger before my bone cracks.

"Drop it, Jase."

The voice is so close I flinch. An even raggier guy, with long greasy hair and tattered clothes, slaps Jase on the shoulder. "Give the girl her lunch, man."

I ignore the scraggly friend and keep my eyes locked on the guy with a grip on my arm.

Jase grits his teeth and glares.

"What's next, you idiot?" says Jase's friend. "You gonna rip a baby bottle out of some little kid's hand?"

Jase eases up on my wrist long enough for me to jerk it free. I pull the Whopper in close to my chest and back away. Meg sticks to my side, still gripping my arm with both of her hands. Jase turns and shoves his friend hard on the shoulder. The friend just laughs, and the two take off, leaving me with a half-eaten burger warm in my hand.

The Whopper is in my mouth and I'm biting down before I can even think. Hunger turns me into a fiend, and I stuff the sandwich into my mouth with shaking hands, not stopping until there is only one bite left. Meg. I stop, look at my baby sister, and offer her the last little bit. Meg wrinkles her nose and shakes her head. I pop it in my mouth and wonder how long it will take all the nasty germs I just ate to give me a snotty nose or an aching head. Ending up with a life-threatening virus wouldn't be all that great either.

Our bus arrives, and Meg and I step on. I pay for the tickets; bus fare isn't that expensive, but it still leaves us with only a few dollars in change. Not enough to buy much of a lunch. Definitely not enough to buy dinner. I could panhandle more, but I hated begging and never want to do it again. If it's between holding out my hand for a few coins and starving, though, I'll stand in front of the library all day and beg until my arm falls off.

I find us a seat near the back of the bus and settle Meg by the window. She presses her hands and nose against the glass, studying every person that walks by. The day is still beautiful; the sun is so bright and yellow you want to throw your hands over your head and dance in the warmth. Or, that's how I'd feel if Mom were sitting right next to us and we had full bellies and a safe place to sleep for the night. Our bus pulls away, and Meg keeps her face right up to the glass. I turn away from the window and stare straight ahead, not seeing a single person.

What do I do when we get to Darren's? Saunter up to his door, bang on it, and ask him to please hand over my mom? That scenario is so ridiculous it's laughable, but I need a plan. Call the police? Can they search Darren's place on my say-so? Wouldn't they need some reason to believe Mom was in his apartment?

I try to concentrate, but that burger didn't do a thing to clear the fuzz in my brain. It only made my stomach howl for the full meal deal with fries, a large chocolate milkshake, and a stack of chocolate chip cookies thrown in for dessert. The bus rumbles along, picking up new passengers and dropping more off. It's slow, it's boring, but I don't mind.

My plan has to be as safe as possible. Meg and I survived a week living in a car and a night alone on the street. I can't be dumb now and lead us right into the jaws of disaster. I'm so wrapped up in my thoughts that I don't notice Darren's apartment complex until Meg pokes me in the side.

"Aren't we going to Darren's?"

My arm shoots up in time to pull the cord. The driver rolls into the next stop, and the doors open with a whoosh. Meg and I shuffle forward and step off the bus onto the sidewalk. Darren parks his pickup in the slot right in front of his place, so if the truck is there, we'll know he's home. I'm not worried he'll spot us, because he always keeps his blinds drawn.

Meg and I walk down the street until we get to the first building in the complex. A woman steps out of her home carrying a baby in an infant carrier. She walks over to her car, buckles the baby in, and drives away. Nobody else is around, but that's normal. Sundays are always quiet, with people staying tucked into their apartments, enjoying a few extra hours of sleep and a lazy day at home.

I keep walking, dragging Meg along with me. What if Darren comes out and sees us? Would he take us too? I'd kick and scream and wake up the entire apartment complex. If somebody saw him drag us into his place, hopefully they'd call the cops. Once the police showed up, they'd have a reason to search Darren's apartment. Perfect, except that scenario counts on somebody witnessing the kidnapping and calling it in—a big *if* in a place where people try to stay out of everyone else's life.

Darren's truck is in the parking space right in front of his place, which means he's home. As I expected, the blinds on the windows are closed even though it's a bright, sunny day. When we lived there, Mom would pull up the blinds in the morning and let the light stream in. The apartment would look bright and cheerful and halfway decent until Darren closed everything down so he could watch TV. Even in the summer he had a way of turning his apartment into a dark, dreary hole.

Meg squeezes my hand with both of hers. "I'm scared."

"I am too, Meg. Really scared."

I turn back to Darren's apartment. If I draw him out, maybe I can race in, lock the front door, and get Mom out the back. Ideas buzz around me like a swarm of bees. I toss most of my ideas out, but I grab onto bits and pieces until I've got a plan. Darren takes better care of his truck than anything else he owns. That has to be the key.

Meg wraps her arms around my stomach and presses her face against my sweatshirt. She should be racing around the playground on this beautiful, quiet Sunday. She should be curled up on the couch with her stack of books or playing with her dollhouse, not worrying about what happened to her mom or where she's going to sleep for the night.

I take a deep breath, kneel in front of her, and outline my plan. I go over every detail I can think of, partly so Meg knows what's coming and partly because I need to get everything squared up and tidy. It may work. It may not.

I put both hands on her shoulders. "Do you remember your little hideout in the bushes, where you played pretend?"

Meg nods and points at a small clump of shrubs that separate the apartment buildings. "Those?"

"Yes," I say. "You can hide in there while I find out if Darren has taken Mom."

Meg stares up at me with eyes so big and watery they look like deep blue puddles. "But what if Darren grabs you too? What if he takes you into his apartment and you're gone?"

"Then run to George and Edith's and knock really loud so they can hear you."

Meg's face crumples. "But they yell at us for every little noise and say mean things about you and Mommy, and they frown at me like they hate me even though I always tried my very best to be good."

I pull my little sister close and give her a hug. "They know you, and George will be more than glad to call the police for you." I lean back and look into her eyes. "And that's what you ask them to do—call the police. Understand?"

"But why can't I stay with you, Mattie?" Meg blinks back her tears. "Darren would have lots more trouble grabbing two of us."

"The biggest help is for me to know you're safe. Plus, you can look out and see me the whole time." I give her another big hug. "We've got to be brave, okay?"

I walk Meg over to the shrubs. She looks at me long and hard before getting on her hands and knees and crawling into the little nest she made for herself.

"Be brave," I whisper, "and stay here."

I stand up, cut across the scrap of lawn in front of George and Edith's apartment, and stop on the sidewalk by Darren's pickup. It's one of those big heavy-duty ones with wide black tires and shiny silver hubs. The paint is black and so polished I can see my face in it. Darren constantly washes it, keeping the inside super tidy. He loves it more than anything or anybody, including Mom.

I walk over to the driver's side door and peer inside. I'm hoping to see Mom's backpack, phone, or something to tell me she's been here, but there isn't even a stray candy wrapper in the cab. I try the door. Locked. Darren always locks his truck, but I run around to the passenger's side. That door is locked too.

My plan is to draw Darren out of the apartment, and the only way he'll get far enough away from the front door is to save his truck. I'll convince him that if he doesn't let Mom go, I'll damage his truck so bad he'll be paying repair bills for the next five years.

If Darren doesn't give up Mom with just the threat, I'll scratch the paint with a key or anything else I can find. That will bring him running out the door. Then I'll race toward the apartment, hopefully get in before Darren catches me, and lock the door. It might be enough time for me to get Mom out the back through the sliding glass door. My plan is flimsy. Scary. Even dangerous. But how else are we going to see if Mom is in there?

The more I run through the plan, the faster my heart beats. I dig in the front pocket of my pack and pull out my keys. I've only got two, a car key for Ruby—even though I don't have my license yet—and Darren's apartment key. The idea of scratching the side of Darren's truck with his own house key almost makes me laugh.

I'm so jittery it feels like I've eaten ten giant candy bars and tossed back five supersized Cokes. I look at my phone. The battery icon blinks at me, indicating it's almost dead. I shut my eyes and rail at myself. I sat in the library for almost an hour and never plugged it in. I just sat there useless, with my mind frozen. How could I be so stupid? All week, I've been careful to charge up my phone every chance I got. Never once have I forgotten—not until this morning, when I need it the most. I take a deep breath, open my eyes, and tap in Darren's number.

It rings three times before I get a "This person is no longer accepting your calls."

How stupid of me. Of course he blocked my number. Meg and I are nothing to him. Why wouldn't he block my calls? Especially if he's the kind of person who would kidnap Mom.

I put my phone back in my pocket. *Okay*, I think, *new plan*. I've got to go right to his door and bang until he opens it.

I run through the whole scenario like I'm watching a cop show on TV. Knocking on his door puts me in a vulnerable position, but if I'm quick enough to get back to Darren's truck, I can drag his key down the side, scratching up his paint. He'll be so worried about his car, he won't be thinking about Mom.

I walk toward Darren's door like I'm one of King Arthur's knights heading toward a fire-breathing dragon. Slow and cautious, but strong and skillful. Ready to dodge at an instant. I hold my keys out in front of me like a sword. Darren can't see me, but acting like a dragon slayer gives me confidence.

Touching the door makes my stomach roll over. I swallow, afraid I'll be sick and ruin any hope I have of getting Mom out.

Before I knock, I glance across the scrap of front yard to the shrubs at the end of the building. Meg is too hidden for me to see her, but just knowing she's there gives me strength. I shake my head to clear away my fears, ball up my fist, and bang on the door.

"Darren." I hit the door again and again. "I know you're in there." A week's worth of stress and worry pours into my fist. I bang harder. "You low-life, bottom-feeding pig. Open the door."

I pound and pound. "I'm going for your truck." I let out every bit of rage I feel for the guy who dumped us in the street. "Look through your window if you don't believe me."

I hold up my keys and rattle them even though Darren can't hear it. "I'll scratch that big, fancy truck of yours until you can't even recognize it."

I keep pounding. Keep yelling. George sticks his head out the next window and yells, "Shut up, for God's sake!"

I ignore him and pound the door again. "Here I go, Darren, right for—"

The door flies open. Darren grabs my right wrist, twists my arm behind me, and rips the keys out of my hand. I don't have a chance to kick or run or even scream.

"What do you want, Mattie?"

He's behind me, so I can't see him, but I can smell the beer on his breath. I try to twist out of his grasp, but the more I wiggle and squirm, the tighter he grips me. Pain shoots from my shoulder all the way to the tips of my fingers. My wrist is already sore from fighting for the Whopper, and my arm aches like it will snap if I keep trying to wrench it free. I stop struggling.

Meg scrambles out of her hiding place and races down the sidewalk. When she gets up to us, she kicks Darren hard in the leg, over and over again. Darren growls but doesn't let go.

"Go to George and Edith's, Meg," I yell. "Ask them to call the police."

Meg spins away, but Darren grabs her just as she tries to slip behind him.

"What do you think you're doing?" he says.

Meg's foot flies out and lands another kick to Darren's shin. "Give us our mommy, you big bully," she yells. "Give us our mommy!"

Darren looks shocked, "What are you talking about?" He drops my arm so suddenly I fall forward, stumbling to keep from landing on the cement.

I swing around, my left fist flying. He steps back and dodges to the side. My knuckles connect with nothing but air.

Darren leans over and grasps Meg by the shoulders. "Where is your mom? Why isn't she with you?"

Meg quits wiggling, sticks out her chin, and crumples her nose. "Because you took her, you old meanie."

My arms drop to my sides. Prickles of pain shoot through my right one, making my hand tingle. "If you hurt her, I'll tear you apart," I say. My threat is stupid. Childish. There's no way I can overpower him, and we both know it.

Darren lets go of Meg, straightens up, and turns to me. "Mattie." He pauses, studying me with super sad eyes. "I haven't seen or heard from your mom since you left."

Reality sinks in. Cold and hard and scary. He's telling the truth.

"I shouldn't have hit your mom." He looks away. "I was drunk. It was stupid. It was bad, and I'm sorry."

I pictured him a monster. Built him up to be a kidnapper, a criminal to be sent to prison forever. He'd never acted that terrible in the two and a half years we'd known him, but I made him into a demon. A hateful, awful, ugly thing. Now I see he's just a drunk and an abuser with too many problems of his own.

Meg tilts her head up to study him. "Mommy's not here?"

Darren shakes his head.

Meg's disappointment is so apparent that her whole body slumps. I can barely look at her. She doesn't ask the question, but I can read it in her eyes because it's my question too. If Mom's not here, where is she? I reach over and take Meg's hand. She melts into me, the two of us so used to being together we can hardly function alone.

Darren's eyes look dull and gray. His sharp features sag. The lines in his face turn into deep crevices. "But where's Rita?"

I press my lips together and shrug my shoulders. "We don't know, but we'll find her." I turn to go.

"Don't go." Darren grabs my arm. "You can't leave without telling me what happened."

A fresh wave of pain stabs me in the shoulder. I give him the quick version, telling him about last night, not the whole week.

"You've reported her missing?" His eyes search my face.

I shake my head. "We've got to go, Darren."

"Stay here. In the apartment." He lets go of my arm and glances at Meg. "Please."

As if we're one person, with one mind, Meg and I turn to leave. Darren steps in front of us, his eyes never leaving my face. "What do you need, Mattie?" His voice cracks with emotion. "Please. Let me help."

"Food." The word pops out of my mouth before I can pull it back.

I don't want anything from him. He caused all of this. All the hurt and anxiety we've gone through. All these awful things are his fault. Or at least, he's easy to blame for everything that's ever gone wrong in our lives.

And now Mom is gone. Lost. Living through who knows what kind of hell. Darren's eyes tell me he knows what he's done, but I can't forgive him. Not now, and maybe not ever.

"Wait." That's all he says before rushing into his apartment.

Meg and I stand on the sidewalk and look through the open door. The living room is a wreck. Beer cans, empty pizza boxes, and McDonald's wrappers litter the coffee table and couch. A pile of dirty clothes covers the chair.

Darren hurries back with a plastic grocery bag in his hands. "Here. It's all I've got."

For an instant, I think about throwing it in his face—showing him I'm brave and strong enough without his charity—but that'd be adding stupid on top of stupid. I take the bag. "Thanks."

Darren takes his wallet out of his back pocket and pulls out every bill he has. He holds them out to me, but I don't take his money. He shakes the bills. "Take it. Please, take it."

There is so much pain in his face. So much hurt in his eyes. He needs me to take it, maybe just to relieve his guilt. I open my palm—this is for Meg and me, not for him—and Darren places the money in it. I stuff the bills deep into the pocket of my jeans.

Darren shoves his hand back into his pocket and takes out all the change he has. He turns to Meg and offers it to her. Meg glances at me. I nod. She holds out both of her hands and Darren dumps it in.

Meg stares at the money before offering it up to me. "You keep it, Mattie." I take the coins out of her hands and slide them into my other pocket.

Meg glares at Darren. "You better not get rid of my doll-house, Darren, because I'm coming back for it."

Darren nods. "It's still in your room, Meg. I'll keep it until you come." He leans toward me, his eyes burning with emotion. "I'll unblock your number so you can reach me. You call. Anytime. I'll come and get you. Understand?"

Those are the kindest words Darren ever said to me. Does that mean he cares about us? Did he always? Or is this sudden softness just heaps and heaps of guilt? Meg and I grab hands and head for the bus stop.

Darren stands on the sidewalk, watching us. When we get to the end of the building, he says, "Call me. I'll come," before stepping into his apartment and closing the door.

CHAPTER TWENTY

A JAR OF PEANUT BUTTER that's almost full, half a loaf of bread, a bag of potato chips with the top rolled down, and one dried-out doughnut is not the healthiest of lunches, but it's food. I'm grateful to Darren, even though I don't want to admit it. Meg and I sit on the bench at the bus stop and plow right through the doughnut and potato chips. I twist the lid off the peanut butter jar so we can dip our fingers in and scoop out the rich, creamy treat, popping it straight into our mouths.

Our bus arrives. I screw the top back on the peanut butter and pull change out of my pocket. Meg and I step on, find a seat near the front, and settle in for a trip back to the library. Where else can we go? At least there, Meg can sit and read and I can charge my phone while I figure out what comes next.

I slump on the bus seat, sad and tired. My nervous energy is gone. Wasted on Darren. Used up on a dead-end, childish idea that I should have known was ridiculous from the beginning. I am embarrassed at my flailing attempts to find Mom.

The bus turns onto River Road and heads downtown. I stare out the window, letting the landscape blur together with no form or structure. My mind is groggy, but I work at pulling my thoughts together. We're near St. Vinnie's, where Mom works with Carly and Jen. I don't have their phone numbers, but if I could talk to them, they might know where Mom took Ruby for repairs.

Did we go by the bus stop closest to the store? I glance around, but it takes me a minute to orient myself and see we're a couple of blocks past it. We could get off at the next stop, but we'd either have to walk the extra distance or wait for the next bus to take us back to the right stop.

If I knew Carly or Jen was working, it would be worth the trek, but if they aren't there, I would waste valuable time. The minutes I bought for my phone still haven't been added, and I don't want to use the last of my data time to look up the phone number for St. Vinnie's.

Because of my indecision, the bus is now several blocks away. I lean back against the bus seat. When I get to the library, I'll look up the phone number for St. Vinnie's. Carly or Jen should be able to take a call, especially if I say it's an emergency.

I close my eyes and let the motion of the bus lull me back into a state of half-consciousness. Darren gave us enough money to keep looking for Mom, so I should be relieved, but instead, a huge wave of sadness washes over me.

What if spending this long, weary day is the last time Meg and I have together? The sun will set, and if we haven't found

Mom, Meg and I will go into foster care. The caseworkers won't have any trouble finding a home for a cute little girl with good manners, but what about a teenager?

I try to concentrate on what to do next, but it's useless. I open my palm and look at Jack's phone number. The blue ink is smeared and faded, the numbers illegible, but it doesn't matter. I know them by heart.

Jack's easy manner and the softness of his voice when he talked to me were a lifetime ago—so far away it's hard to remember if they were real or just stories from another world or a different time in history. Still, the warmth I felt with him hangs on, seeping through my body and deep into my very bones.

Do I text Jack and thank him for lunch yesterday? Until I find Mom safe and alive, my life is shattered. Is it fair to drag him into this chaos, or do I fade away, maybe never to see him again?

Jack offered to help if I needed anything, so programming his number into my phone is a safety precaution for Meg and me, not just a personal one. I slide my cell out of the front pocket of my pack and stare at it for a long time. If his cell number is easy to call, I don't have to think. I can just tap the screen if Meg and I are desperate. My fingers fly across the numbers, programming Jack into my phone—and maybe into my life.

I go one step further and tap out a text. *Thanks for lunch yesterday. The food and company meant a lot to Meg and me. Mattie.* If I hit send, Jack has my phone number and can call or text me. Do I want that? Sharing my number with Jack makes me more vulnerable to him. Can I handle the pressure, or will I lose sight of my own goals? Before I change my mind, I hit send, then stare at the screen long after my message has flown through the air to land in Jack's back pocket.

Jack doesn't respond, which I'm glad about. He's busy, and I don't have to lie and say we're fine, or spill out the sad tale of my life and drag him down into my problems. I slide my phone back into my pack, zip it in, and hook the straps through my arms even though it sits on my lap, just to make sure it can't be stolen.

I squeeze my fingers over the inky smear on my hand, lean my head back, and close my eyes. I don't wake until the driver stops the bus and yells, "End of the line! Everybody off."

CHAPTER TWENTY-ONE

MEG AND I GO BACK to the library's young adult section. The area is quiet, with only a few kids at the computers and a couple more searching through the stacks. Meg climbs onto the window seat with her books like it's the couch in our living room.

I go over to the computers and look up the phone number for St. Vinnie's, dialing it into my phone. It rings a couple of times before it's answered by a guy with a rapid, "St. Vincent de Paul. How can I help you?"

"Hi." I duck behind a bookshelf and try to keep my voice low. "Is Carly or Jen working today? It's an emergency. I need to talk to one of them."

The guy doesn't hesitate. "Let me check."

I glance around while I wait, nervous that precious minutes are ticking off my phone. A couple of kids are hanging out in the back corner, and an older woman looks at the books on the stack across from me. I turn my back to her so I won't draw her attention.

The guy comes back on the cell. "Jen moved to Portland. Carly was supposed to work today, but she had to take her brother to Medford. Sorry."

"Thanks."

I go back to Meg, plug in my phone, and drop next to her, leaning against the window. Disappointment seeps through me. Why do I get my hopes up? I should know better by now; every time I get an idea of how or where to find Mom, the plan is ruined before I get anywhere. I stare off into space and try to think through every tiny detail from yesterday.

My phone dings, and I reach down and pick it up. Jack. More decisions. Do I respond? Maybe I should wait until Meg and I have found Mom and I am back to living a seminormal life.

I open his message. *Glad to see your text. I'm at Gram's house with parents and family. Mom threatened to take my phone for a month if I took it out of my pocket so had to wait for a chance. Are you okay?*

Tears spring to my eyes, and my mouth quivers. Jack lives that perfect life with two parents, a grandmother, and a houseful of family—the life that I want so badly I dream about it. Does Jack know he's lucky to have a family to turn to if something goes wrong? Does he appreciate the roof over his head and the money in his pocket? I swallow the ache in my heart and avoid his question. *Where are you that your mom won't catch you?*

Jack texts, *In the bathroom* ☺

A picture of Jack sitting on a toilet lid in his grandmother's house with his thumbs flying across his phone dances in my head and brings a twitch of a smile to the corner of my mouth. *Go back to your family. I can't talk now.*

Jack's response is quick, *Are you okay?*

I stare at the text and wonder if I should lie, just evade the truth, or not text back at all. *I'll call if I need help.*

Jack replies, *Good. I'm here.*

I plug my phone back into the wall and sit back against the warm window. Texting Jack broke my concentration, and I vow not to open another message or take a call until I've exhausted every possibility of finding Mom.

Mapping out where Mom was during her day and what she did might help me focus. I reach for my pack and dig around until I find my notebook and a pencil. Mom left work on time. I draw little pictures and diagram her route. I make a graphic list along the side, crossing out the hospital, a car accident, and Darren kidnapping her. I sketch a garage near the 7-Eleven and Mom walking to it.

Picturing Mom walking along a dark street all alone sends my heart racing. How often did she tell me not to get caught out by myself like that? A stranger could have grabbed her on the way to the garage.

I lean forward on the window seat, suddenly alert. The garage. Meg glances at me, but I don't do anything but stare straight ahead. I'm so excited and nervous I can hardly breathe. The mechanic. Why didn't I think of the garage before? Mom called somebody to work on Ruby. He might be the one who kidnapped her.

Officer Rodriguez told Mom to get Ruby fixed right away. My fingers clutch at the notebook in my lap. Mom would have to take Ruby somewhere close to her job so she could drop her off on a break and pick her up after work. My excitement grows so quickly I can hardly keep from screaming. I've got to check every garage close to the 7-Eleven.

"Stay here, Meg," I whisper. "I'm going over to the computers to check on something."

My fingers move across the keyboard so fast I make a ton of mistakes and have to remind myself to slow down. My search gives me three possible garages, maybe four. All have websites, but each lists their hours from eight to five, Monday through Friday. No Saturday hours. No emergency numbers. I copy their numbers anyway and hurry back to my phone. I squat down and tap in the first number. After five rings, an answering machine kicks in, listing the hours the garage is open and asking the caller to leave a message at the beep. No emergency number. I hang up and call the next garage on my list. Same drill. No emergency numbers. I try every garage and come up with nothing.

I sit back on the window seat beside Meg and go over my map. I start at the beginning of Mom's day, when she kissed us goodbye and walked into work. I draw a little picture of Ruby, with Mom heading into the 7-Eleven and Meg and me hanging out in Ruby reading stories until we caught the bus to the mall.

Off on a tangent, I draw Meg and I going to the mall on the bus. My step-by-step reasoning gets sidetracked with Jack taking us to lunch. I quickly draw a picture of Meg and I going back to the library and bring my focus back to Mom. To concentrate on her day, not mine.

I draw a picture of Mom at work, standing behind the counter fitting calls to garages in between customers. She'd find all the garages were closed like I did, so what would she do then? The internet? Craigslist? Mom uses the website all the time for good deals on everything from kid's clothes to furniture to laptop computers. She'd be looking for somebody cheap. Somebody open on Saturday. But does Craigslist even advertise for mechanics?

I hurry back to the computers and open Craigslist. Under "Services," I click on "Automotive." It was yesterday, so I scroll back a day and there it is: "Cheap fast auto repair. Twenty-four-hour service, seven days a week." I stare at the phone number. Now what? Call? Ask the mechanic if he happens to have a Rita Rollins bound and gagged in his back room?

Kids my age have their own cars. Not me, but he wouldn't know that. What if I call him and pretend I need a mechanic? He'd give me the address and tell me to drive to his garage. I could take the bus and check out the place from a distance. I wouldn't have to go up to him; I'd watch the garage until he got tired of waiting for me. Then, when he wasn't there, I could break in and look for Mom.

This guy is no bumbling hothead like Darren. If the mechanic kidnapped Mom, he might be a murderer, a rapist, or even a psychopath. The back of my neck tingles, and pinpricks of fear shoot through my body. This guy could be deadly.

I input the mechanic's phone number and look up the Eugene Police Department as well. If I find Mom or evidence of where she is, I'll need to call them quickly, and if I'm not any closer to knowing where Mom is by the end of the day, I have to call them anyway.

I program the police department number into my phone and go back to Meg. Late-afternoon sun still brightens the day. Looking out the window at the slanting rays should make me feel warm, or even hot. It doesn't. Instead, a cold certainty sits in the pit of my gut. Mom's hurt. If this mechanic is criminal enough to kidnap her, he's bad enough to do almost anything.

One fact is certain: Meg can't come with me. I wasn't worried about taking her to Darren's place because she could stay safe in her little hideout. If Darren dragged me into his apartment, George and Edith were right there, and Meg could get help.

Taking her with me to the garage is too dangerous. Meg and I don't know the area or the situation—if I got in trouble, she wouldn't know where to go or how to get help.

Mom's friend Carly is out of town, and I don't have her phone number anyway. My friend Lilly takes care of her siblings all the time, so I trust her; plus, she could borrow her parents' car and come to the library to get Meg.

My phone sits at my feet, plugged into the wall socket. I squat beside it and send a text to Lilly. *Could you watch Meg for the next couple of hours? I've got something I have to do and she can't come with me.*

Lilly texts back almost instantly. *Sorry. I'm at Tanner's. His parents are gone. Wooooo!!! Maybe next time?*

I swallow my disappointment and text back, *Thanks anyway.*

My phone rests in my hand, still plugged into the wall. Jack is my only option. Should I call him? He won't be satisfied to watch Meg without knowing what I intend to do. I need time to think, so I keep my phone plugged in and sit back beside Meg.

Tracking the mechanic without a way to call the police would be dumb, so that means my battery needs to be charged. I stare out the window. The sun's rays slant across the street outside in those long slivers of light that tell me whatever happens needs to happen soon. I give myself fifteen more minutes and hope that's enough time to charge my phone.

Meg hands me one of her favorite picture books and gives me a sad, pleading look that crushes my heart. She knows that sitting in our favorite window seat at the library on a warm and sunny afternoon is only temporary. For now, this is our home, but it won't be for long.

I read three picture books and don't pay a bit of attention to the words. Instead, I ache for my baby sister. Meg's grown up too much for a little kid. In one week, her face has gone from an innocent first-grader with a sassy grin and twinkling blue eyes to a world-weary girl. A girl with sadness behind her eyes and a smile not quite as wide or as soft as it was a few days ago.

I finish the third book, pick up my phone, and glance at the time. Sixteen minutes have gone by. I'm not worried anymore. Just resigned.

"Time to go, Megsy," I whisper.

Meg doesn't even ask me where we're headed. She gathers the library books, leaving them in a neat little stack on the window seat, and slips on her backpack. We go to the bathroom, get a drink, and head outside. I hesitate on the sidewalk.

Cars buzz by, filling the air with the din of traffic all in a hurry to get somewhere. The street is bathed in that soft white light that makes the world seem sleepy—that glowing end-of-the-day look that reminds people it's time to go home. Time to cook dinner, set the table, and do homework. I shake away the sadness pressing on me and bend down to Meg.

"I found the name of a mechanic." I run my hand over her hair, pushing a long strand away from her face. "He may be the one fixing Ruby. He may be the one who has Mom." I take a deep breath and blow it out in a rush. "I'm going to call him and see if I can find out where he works. Maybe that will give us a clue about what happened to Mom."

Meg looks up at me with dark eyes, but she doesn't say anything or ask any questions. She knows this is the beginning of more tough stuff to come.

I take another deep breath and tap in the number. It rings and rings and rings. I'm about to end the call when the connection goes through and a man's voice says, "Yeah?"

I'm too scared to say a word. Instead, I stand in the middle of the sidewalk and watch the traffic whiz by.

"Anyone there?" the voice says.

"I…I saw your ad." Getting a couple of words out helps the rest of them flow. "On…on Craigslist." I take another breath and rush on. "I need a mechanic. A…a cheap mechanic. To fix my car."

The guy laughs into the phone. "Okay?"

I glance at Meg. "I just don't have a lot of money right now." The truth. The absolute truth.

"What's wrong with your car?"

I study the cars parked beside the curb and try to think of a problem that makes sense. "The…the lights." Words tumble into my mouth. "They click off when I'm driving. Like at night when I really need them." I pause to gather my story into something halfway believable. "I'm taking off on a trip tomorrow morning, so I can't wait for a garage to open up."

"Does anything else go off when the lights go out?" he asks.

Here's the sticky part. The point where I could tip him off, and he'd know I don't really need my car fixed. If I mess up and my words don't make sense, he'll be alert and wary, and who knows what he'll do to Mom—if he has her. "I haven't noticed," I say. "I was so freaked out when the lights quit that I didn't check anything else."

There's a pause. I don't know if I should say anything more or just wait. Finally, the guy says, "I could look at it." He pauses again. "Tell me where you live."

Now I'm scared. Really scared. I try to keep my voice steady. "I'll come there. What's the address of your garage?"

"Look, Miss," he says, "I'm doing you a favor by coming to your place."

My hand grips the phone so tight I'm afraid I'll crush it. "I don't want to give my home address to a stranger."

This time the pause is even longer. "Bring it by then." He gives me the address and directions to get there. I jot it all on the front cover of my notebook. "When are you coming?" he says.

The address isn't anywhere close. "Maybe forty-five minutes?" I say.

"I'll be waiting."

CHAPTER TWENTY-TWO

MY HAND SHAKES, AND MY insides turn watery and loose. I grip
the phone tighter and squat next to my little sister. "I need
to check out the garage, and I can't take you with me, Meg."

Meg's face is pinched with worry. "It's too dangerous," I
say. "I'll call Jack, the friend that bought us lunch yesterday,
and he'll take care of you while I'm gone."

Meg stares back at me. "No." She throws down that one
little word, bold and defiant. Her lips press into a straight line;
her eyes blaze with determination. "No, Mattie. You can't
leave me. I won't let you."

I swallow the sour taste in my mouth. "You liked Jack,
and you'll only be with him for a couple of hours until I can
check out the garage."

Meg's voice doesn't waver. "It doesn't matter that I liked
him." She emphasizes each word, making sure I understand.
"If you make me go with him, I'll kick and scream and cry

and people will call the police. Then you'll have to tell them what you're doing, and they will stop you."

"Meg." My voice is loaded with fear for her safety. "You have got to listen to me."

Meg looks at me with a ferocity I have never seen. "No, I don't. I will hide someplace where I can see you, just like at Darren's, but you are not leaving me."

I stand and glare at my sister, hoping size gives me power. "I can't take you, Meg. I don't *dare* take you."

Meg lifts her chin. "I am not a little girl, Mattie. I can call the police if that me…me…me…"

"Mechanic," I say.

"That mechanic guy grabs you like Darren did."

We stare at each other, our feelings of love and need so raw I feel naked and exposed. I press my lips together, jerk my eyes away, and dig my phone out of my pack. "I'm calling Jack."

Meg crosses her arms in such a dramatic way that I'd laugh if I wasn't so afraid for her. "Go ahead. Call him. But when he comes, I'll scream and yell, and you know I will, Mattie. You know I will."

I hit Jack's number and ignore the anger on Meg's face and the fire in her eyes.

Jack's phone rings and keeps on ringing. The sick, sour taste of failure fills my mouth. Why didn't I ask him for help when we were texting? Why did I wait so long, thinking I could handle finding Mom by myself? Pride? Fear of Jack taking over my life? Jack told me he couldn't pull out his phone or he'd lose it. If I had a punching bag, I'd beat my fists against it until my fingers were bloody.

Jack's voice tells me, "Jack. Leave a message."

How do I explain a need so far out of his normal? "Could use some help," I say. "I'll send a text."

A car drives so close to the curb it startles me. I pull my phone away from my ear and drop my hand to my side. Our chance to find Mom slides away with the sun. If I don't go to the garage now then I might as well turn us into the police.

Meg hunches forward and glares. "You are not leaving me."

I sigh, exhausted with her badgering. "You can come part way, but when Jack calls or texts, you're going with him."

Meg grabs my hand and drags me down the street until we're standing in front of the map posted outside the bus station. I tap out a one-handed text to Jack. *Can you come and get Meg?*

Meg stares up at the routes even though she's too short to see much. "Where is the garage?"

I give in and show her, running my finger along the streets and bus routes. "It's out on the fringes of town, but we only need one bus."

Meg glances around at the bus stops and points when she sees the right number. "Over there."

Meg races to the right spot, waving her hand at me to hurry up. The bus doesn't arrive for ten minutes, but we don't talk the whole time we wait. We just stand, hand in hand, until it drives up and slides into its slot.

The address for the garage is near the edge of town. I don't know the area, and the farther we travel, the more worried I get. Houses disappear. Stores and shops turn into warehouses, storage units, and unmarked buildings. It's Sunday, so everything is quiet and deserted. This is an industrial area, not a place where I can yell for help and a small army will show up to rescue me.

I lean my head against the seat and close my eyes. My plan is full of holes, what ifs, and maybes. Even if the mechanic took Mom, why would he keep her at the garage where he works? It's stupid, but what are the alternatives to going there and finding out?

I could call the police—turn it over to people who know what they're doing—and let them launch the search for Mom. That would be a whole lot easier and way less scary, but it's late on a Sunday afternoon. They'll get Meg and me settled with a foster family before they even think about Mom. They might not get a real investigation going until tomorrow, but if I had a tiny scrap of evidence against the mechanic, maybe I could get them to investigate tonight. Wouldn't they at least stop by the garage and take a look around?

My phone dings. I fumble with the zipper on my pack, pull out my cell, and open a text from Jack. *Love to watch Meg. Where do I meet you?*

I tap, *We're on a bus to 3940 West Second Avenue in West Eugene*, and send it off, holding my phone while I wait for Jack's answer.

Our bus passes another block, drawing Meg and me closer to our stop and maybe Mom. My cell throbs in my hand. *I'm still at Gram's in Springfield. Mom and Dad drove us over so I've got to drag them away or leave them without a car.*

Tears spring to my eyes. What if he has to take his parents home or they won't let him have the car? Why am I so stubborn about finding Mom on my own? I write, *Wait a couple of blocks away until you hear from me. I'll text when I know more.*

Meg sits beside me with her backpack on her lap. My phone hums with another text from Jack. *What are you planning? Please don't do anything crazy okay? Promise?*

My whole makeshift plan *is* crazy, so what can I say? Before I tuck my phone in my pocket, I tap the icon for my service plan to see if the minutes I bought have been added. The information make me feel sick to my stomach. My call minutes are down to nineteen, and my texting stands at thirteen. The long calls to the hospital, dead-end ones to the garages, and even the one to St. Vinnies ate up more time than I thought, plus I've been texting like I had unlimited time.

I slide my phone in my pocket, and stare out the window. The minutes on my cell plan will cover a few more calls and texts, but then what? If the company doesn't add more time in the next few hours, we're in deep trouble.

Before I'm ready, it's time to get off the bus. I pull the cord, even though I want to stay in its safety—riding right through the night and into tomorrow—just so we never have to face what's coming.

Meg and I step off the bus in front of a row of self-storage units, all with bright orange doors and surrounded by a tall ironwork fence. Across the street is a tire shop, a plumbing store advertising a sale on sinks, and a place to rent tools. None of the businesses are open.

"Are you sure this is where you want to go?" says the bus driver.

I turn to face her. "Thirty-Nine Forty West Second Avenue?"

The driver points down a side street. "Should be down there," she says, "but it's pretty odd for you to get off out here this late on a Sunday afternoon."

I paste a smile across my face. "Mom's waiting for us at a garage." The truth, sort of.

The bus driver waves, pulls the door closed, and drives away. Meg and I stand on the sidewalk, holding hands. I study the storage units, hoping to see someone unloading a truck or digging through their stuff. Each orange door is shut tight, and there are no cars or people or movement in any direction.

I have never felt so lost and alone. Last night outside the library didn't even feel this bad. At least then there were people walking by, cars driving on the streets, and businesses that stayed open later into the night. Here there is no one. The rest of Eugene is so far away that Meg, me, and the mechanic down the street—a guy who might turn out to be a kidnapper—could be the only people left on Earth.

We walk a block away from the main road before I get so nervous I can't take another step. What if this is not the mechanic that worked on Mom's car? What if I'm endangering Meg and me for nothing? I was wrong about Darren, so I could be wrong about this guy too.

"Let's get off the sidewalk, Meg." I glance around, looking for a route to the garage that doesn't put us out in the open.

A string of plain metal buildings lines both sides of the street. There are no lights in the windows facing the asphalt parking lots and no doors standing ajar as if someone was inside.

Signs hang over the doorways with names of businesses. Some doors are narrow and others are wide, as if they lead to a garage or a warehouse where big trucks come and go. A few businesses take up the whole building, but others have multiple signs tacked over individual doors. If we get on the same side of the street as the garage and stay closer to the building walls, we won't be quite so visible.

I point across the street. "Over there, Meg."

Meg and I clasp hands and run across the street and through the paved parking area in front of the building. We don't stop until we touch the metal wall. I let go of Meg's hand, turn around, and lean my back against the building. Meg imitates everything I do. I stay there a moment, catching my breath. We're far enough away that we don't need to slide along the wall, so we walk, sticking close enough to the buildings to keep ourselves out of open view.

I check the numbers over the doors as we pass them. Thirty-eight forty. Thirty-eight fifty. We keep moving from business to business until I see thirty-eight ninety in big block letters painted over a doorway. I pull out my phone and check the time. It's been almost an hour since I called. The mechanic is waiting for us.

My plan isn't to confront him. That would be foolish—maybe even suicidal—and could put Meg in terrible danger. All I want is to see Ruby so I know this is the right mechanic. Then I can call the police and let them handle the dangerous stuff.

We move across the front of the building to a narrow driveway separating buildings thirty-eight ninety and thirty-nine hundred. I study the parking areas in front of the next two buildings. No Ruby.

Every other garage I've seen has tons of cars parked out front. Sometimes every square inch of their parking lots are filled with vehicles. So why don't I see any here?

Finding Ruby parked in front would be ideal. I could call the police, and they could come out and question the guy. Even if the mechanic didn't kidnap Mom, he might have information that could help us. Mom would have called him to check on Ruby. The mechanic could give us clues to when and where Mom was when she disappeared. By then, the police would be into the case and would keep right on looking for Mom and not leave their search until Monday morning.

I don't say a word to Meg, just point down the driveway toward the back of the building. Meg nods and follows me. We step into a wide alley. The backs of businesses on the next street face us, and dumpsters sit next to back doors. Nobody is around. I glance toward the garage. No cars. No Ruby.

Our beautiful sunny day has deepened to dusk, with shadows blending together from soft gray to deep charcoal. Meg and I inch forward, hugging the wall until we're standing behind the first dumpster.

Why have I brought Meg so close to the garage? Jack said he'd come, yet I charge on, unable to rein in my anxiety. Should I text him? See if he's close?

My phone rings. I jump, so startled by the noise my knees threaten to give out. Mom? I stuff my hand in my pocket and pull out my phone, staring at the number.

Meg grabs my arm. "Mommy?"

I shake my head and whisper, "The mechanic." Could he hear the ring from inside and two doors away? That's not possible, is it?

Meg whispers, "I'm scared."

"I know, honey," I whisper back. "But we're late. He probably wants to know why." My stomach rolls over. If I don't answer the call, he could suspect something. Would he hurt Mom because he got mad that we stood him up? Another ring.

I press the call button and pull the phone to my ear. My mouth is too dry to say hello. I just wait.

"You're late," says the mechanic.

I swallow, trying to make my throat work. "I...I had more car trouble and I...my car won't start and...I can't get there. I'm sorry." I take a breath and keep my voice low, trying not to sound like I'm whispering. "It must be a bigger problem than I thought." I remember my story about taking a trip and add, "I'm going to take the bus. For my trip. A bus instead of the car."

The mechanic hangs up on me. I stare at the phone in my hand for several seconds before I shove it into my pocket. Did my words sound believable? Maybe he's just disgusted that I wasted his time.

I try to be rational. The guy could have ditched Ruby and taken Mom almost anywhere. Then again, Mom might be one small building away. So close we could yell and she'd hear us. The draw to find her is so strong that I can't think of doing anything different, but I'm not totally stupid. I need backup. A way out if things go bad.

Fear tightens a band around my chest, making it harder and harder for me to breathe. I open my hand, stare at my phone for too long, and finally tap the icon for the police.

"Who are you calling?" whispers Meg.

I push a strand of Meg's hair behind her ear. "The police."

"Eugene Police Department. May I help you?"

Sweat turns my palms damp and slippery. I wipe one hand down the leg of my jeans and grip my phone tighter with the other. Words won't form in my head, even though seconds are ticking off my phone plan. I have to say something, but what?

"May I help you?" My hesitation irritates the woman. Like she thinks I'm a kid making a prank call, tying up the phone line so somebody with a real emergency can't get through.

I keep my voice low, almost a whisper. "Can I speak to Officer Rodriguez please?" Why do I ask for him? Why do I trust a man I only met a couple of times? Another cop might be nicer.

"I'm sorry. He's out of the office right now, but I can take your call."

"No." The word comes out too quickly and even a bit rude. "I mean, can I leave him a message?"

"I'll connect you to his voicemail, but if this is important, you need to give me the information so we can help you."

Officer Rodriguez knows the mess we're in, and yet he didn't haul Meg and me off to children's services and charge Mom with not taking care of her kids. I trust him, but I wonder how long it will take him to check his messages. What if he's on a vacation to Hawaii and doesn't come back to work for days—or even weeks?

"His voicemail please." I wait, gripping the phone in my sweaty palm.

After a couple of clicks and dings, his voice rumbles, "Rodriguez. Leave a message."

I take a deep breath and try to calm myself. "This is Mattie Rollins. I'm calling about my mom, Rita. You met us when we were sleeping in the car, my mom, and my little sister, Meg, and me."

My words catch in my throat, but once I get going they tumble out, tripping over each other. "Mom didn't pick us up outside the library last night, and Meg and I think she's been kidnapped by the mechanic she got to work on Ruby—that's our car—so that's where we are, at Thirty-Nine Forty West Second Avenue. It's a warehouse kind of building, and I'm going to peek in the window to see if I can get a glimpse of Ruby or Mom." I stop to catch my breath, and then quickly add, "It's four forty-seven on Sunday, November nineteenth. If I don't call you back in one hour, please come look for us."

I end the call. Meg looks at me, her face quiet and sober. I whisper, "I'm going to get closer, Meg, but you have to stay here." I kneel and show her how she can peek between the dumpster and the wall. That way, she can watch me but still stay hidden.

"No matter what happens, I want you to stay right here and be very, very quiet. Do you understand?"

Meg nods.

"At Darren's, you didn't mind me. Will you stay here this time? Promise?"

Meg makes a big X over her heart. "I promise, Mattie."

"Even if the mechanic comes out and grabs me like Darren did, you have to stay here, or you could get hurt, and so could I." I take a pencil out of my backpack and rewrite the address of the garage. I show Meg the numbers and explain each one to make sure she understands.

Meg rolls her eyes and whispers back at me. "I *know* how to read numbers."

I'm so nervous I can hardly talk. "I know," I whisper, "just making sure." I write nine-one-one in big numbers above the address. "If something happens to me, tap these numbers, nine-one-one, tell the person this address, and ask them to send the police." I point to the numbers. "You'll have to stay quiet and hidden until it's safe to make the call, though, understand?"

Meg's sassy look is gone. Her job is important, more important than anything she's ever done, and she knows it. "I'll call them, Mattie. Don't worry."

I bring up Jack's number on my phone and write a text. *Meg is hiding behind a dumpster in the alley behind 3920 West Second Avenue. If I'm not there, take Meg away and make sure the police are on the way to 3940. Do not come after me!*

I hit send, a little afraid my text will freak Jack out so much he'll get into an accident on the way. I hand the phone to Meg and chastise myself for getting Meg into this. Calling the police is too much responsibility for a six-year-old. I should have waited to investigate the garage until she could go with Jack. Caution begs me to listen and stay back, yet I am too anxious to get a glimpse of Ruby or Mom to pay attention.

Meg grabs the sleeve of my sweatshirt and tugs it back and forth. "Don't worry, Mattie. I can tap nine-one-one."

I give Meg a weak smile and stand up, but I'm so charged with fear and doubt I can barely hold myself together. I take a deep breath, blow it out, and peer around the dumpster.

Two windows, evenly spaced with a single back door between them, face the alley. The closest window is lit with a soft yellow light that spills out into the growing dusk. If I pop my head in front of that window, I might be able to spot Ruby or Mom, but it's risky. The mechanic could look out at that very moment and spot me.

I lean my back against the wall of the building. This is stupid. I didn't hear a car leave or the shop's front door slam, so that means he's still in there. I could call the police right now and tell them the whole story, but can they search the garage just because I think the guy's got Mom? I doubt it.

All I need is a glimpse of Ruby or a tiny piece of Mom's clothing. Any little bit of evidence that Mom has been here would be enough to let the cops look through the garage.

I pull myself away from the wall and peer around the dumpster. Every minute that ticks by could make the difference between Mom being alive or not. Sweat beads on my neck and slides down the middle of my back. I slip off my backpack, set it on the pavement beside Meg, and rub my palms down the arms of my sweatshirt. I lean over and whisper to Meg. "You're sure you know what to do?"

Meg repeats every step back to me, ending with "…and then I'll tell the nine-one-one people to come fast because the me—mechanic just grabbed you."

I'm too nervous to speak or even nod, so I wrap my arm around Meg and plant a big kiss on the top of her head. I take a deep breath, let go of my sister, and slip around the dumpster. Walking as quickly and quietly as I can, I hurry across the front of the dumpster until I can press my body against the back wall. I slide along the wall until I pass the windows and door on thirty-nine thirty. I keep going until I'm almost at the window of thirty-nine forty.

I lean against the wall and listen. Nothing. This is such a pitiful plan; I feel like a little kid with only one bad idea. No matter how much I doubt myself, though, I refuse to give up looking for Mom—even if all I have left is this one last attempt. I continue along the wall until I'm close to the window.

Early evening settles over the alley. If I stick my head straight in front of the window, I'll be a dark shadow against the gray light behind me, too easy to spot. I could wait against the wall, let the light fade until everything outside is pitch black. That might work, but it means standing out in the open for way too long.

The sane, rational part of me screams to back away, call the police, and let them handle the whole situation. They are the experts and will know what to do, but law enforcement is also hampered by laws and regulations. If I can find one clue that this is Mom's mechanic, I will race back to Meg and call them.

I ignore reason and let my emotions drive me on. Mom could be a few feet away. If I could reach through the walls, she could even be close enough for me to touch. I take a deep breath and slide a bit farther along the wall until I'm right beside the window. My body is flat against the siding, and my ears are listening for any tiny noise from inside. Nothing.

The back door flies open so hard it bangs against the wall and rattles the metal siding. I jump and nearly cry out before clamping my lips together and swallowing my terror.

Instantly, I see my mistake—one more in a long string of blunders. I should have crept across the back of the building to the far window, not the close one. That way I could run away from Meg. Now, my only chance of escape is to turn around and lead the mechanic right back to my little sister. I press myself flat against the wall and hope he doesn't look my way.

A man steps out the door with a black plastic garbage bag in his hand. I push hard against the wall, but he spots me in an instant. A broad smile spreads across his thin face. He's an average-sized guy with straight brown hair that is cut neat and trim. His jeans are clean, and his plaid shirt hangs over his belt but doesn't look sloppy. He's not very old, maybe thirty or thirty-five, and good-looking. If I saw him on the street, I'd think he was a nice guy with a decent job and a wife, with maybe even a couple of kids.

The mechanic slings the garbage bag into the dumpster and takes a step toward me. "Let me guess." The corner of his mouth curls into a sideways grin. "Your lights blink out."

This guy is totally different than I pictured. The mechanic in my mind had long, stringy hair and scars on his face. He wore greasy clothes, had rips in his jeans and tattoos running down his arms. The mechanic in my imagination made my skin crawl just to look at him. This guy looks like a person women would love to date.

"You're driving along, fine as fine until your lights just aren't there anymore." He says the words with a flare of drama, like he's playing a part in a movie or telling a story. "I waited a whole hour for you."

His words don't scare me—or his looks or smile or even the way he stands with his fingers in his front pockets. None of those things are threatening. His eyes don't even wander over my body, undressing me like some of Darren's friends. With all my fear and worry, am I transforming him into a complete monster, like I did with Darren?

Tension bleeds from my shoulders. Maybe the mechanic fixed Ruby, and maybe he didn't. Doesn't matter. Mom could be anywhere. Just because I got an idea in my head doesn't make it real.

I look deeper into the man's eyes. They're a pale blue, but it's not their color that brings back my fear. The mechanic's eyes are cold and guarded, like he's looking at me behind layers and layers of heavy glass.

Tension climbs back into me. Muscles in my back and neck turn rigid. Sweat beads on my forehead. It's how *ordinary* the man is that makes me nervous and on edge. The curious way he looks at me with his head tipped to the side. The relaxed, easy way he stands while he seems to mentally record every breath I take.

I can't run back the way I came. That would endanger Meg. I step away from the wall, never taking my eyes away from him. "I'm looking for my mom."

"And why should I know anything about your mom?"

The mechanic pulls his hands out of his pockets, holding them away from his sides. He doesn't lunge for me, yet all I can think about is running. I have no evidence, nothing to link this man to Mom, but instinct tells me this is no regular auto mechanic just doing his job. This nice-looking guy is the creep who took my mom.

CHAPTER TWENTY-THREE

MY MUSCLES ACHE TO RUN. Nerves twitch, warning me I'm crazy to stand my ground. My job is to save myself and Meg too, but I've come too far and given up too much to quit now. "Just let Mom go. That's all I want. Just my mom."

The man's eyes never change, just keep studying me with that same calmness. "What if I say your mom isn't here?" He steps away from the dumpster.

He's only one step closer, but the distance between us shrinks from several feet to what feels like inches. "You fixed our car. It's an old, red Subaru." Sweat runs down the side of my face even though the air is cool.

"So?"

"So you were the last one to see her." I push the words out with more strength than I feel. "You took her. You...you...kidnapped her."

The mechanic snorts. "And you're...let me guess. Sherlock Holmes?"

Doubt creeps back into my mind. He's so casual and easy-going, and he acts like finding me pressed against the wall of his garage isn't the least bit crazy. What if this guy has nothing to hide, and all I've been doing is wasting time?

We stand in the fading light of the alley and study each other. My doubts dissolve. The mechanic may be clean, neat, and look like a decent man, but he's not surprised Mom is missing. Any person with a shred of humanity would say, "Your mother is missing? Have you called the police?" An innocent man would be shocked that I am alone. They would offer to help me find her or ask question after question to draw out my story. This guy just stands and watches me.

My mind spins. I can't run toward Meg, so that means sprinting right across his path. I take off before I lose my nerve, angling as far away from the mechanic as I can, hoping I'm fast enough to outrun him.

I don't get ten feet before he lunges, grabs my arms from behind, and shoves me toward the gaping garage door.

I struggle against him, but the guy wrestles me forward. "Monster!" I scream. "Sick, perverted—" He clamps a hand over my mouth and picks me up by my waist with the other.

The mechanic's body presses hard against me. He's strong—all raw muscle, bone, and heartless drive. I kick his shins with my heels, claw at his hands, and throw my weight against his arms. His hands only clamp down tighter. In my panic, I struggle for air and choke on his sweaty smell. He drags me past the door, kicks it closed with his heel, and throws me onto the cement floor.

I scramble to my feet and scurry away from the door. The garage is dim, lit by one light hanging over a cluttered workbench. A double-wide garage door covers most of the front wall. Three cars sit parked at odd angles. The one closest to the workbench is Ruby. I slide that way, keeping my eye on the mechanic standing near the door. He doesn't come after me, but just stands and watches everything I do.

"I'll...I'll scream." My words come out so shaky and soft they sound ridiculously weak. I stand tall and throw the force of my fear behind them. "I'm serious. I'll scream my head off."

"Go ahead." The mechanic gives me that too-relaxed smile, like he's discussing football scores or the weather. "No one's around."

My mouth goes dry. "Someone will hear me."

"Doubt it." He waves his arm at the walls imprisoning me. "The place is insulated, plus no one hangs around on the weekends."

Sweat runs down my face in long, icy streams. "Where's Mom?"

The mechanic nods his head toward an office area with a single room built above it. A staircase leads up the wall to a narrow door. "Up there."

Outside, there was no window that high up—which means there's only one way into that room and one way out. In this big space, this garage full of cars and tools and junk, I've got a fighting chance. Racing to that little room? Trying to rescue Mom? I'd never get up the stairs before he'd get to me.

"Go get her." My command surprises me. It surprises the mechanic too, because he jerks his head back like I landed a punch on his jaw.

I take advantage of the situation and back away until I can lay my hand on Ruby. "You can keep our car." I thump her side. "Just let us go."

The mechanic breaks into laughter, making my head pound. The sound bounces off the walls and metal of the garage and scares me so much my breath gets caught in my throat.

He waves his hand at Ruby. "That piece of junk?" He laughs again. "Not worth the time to process it." His hand stops moving, and his finger points at me like a gun. "Now you. You are worth a lot."

"You're a…a pimp?" I spit the word at him.

"Nope. Too much work. Not enough money." He rubs his fingers together. "I'm a businessman." He points back at me. "And you're young. Black. Pretty." He winks. "Your mom's not worth as much, but you? You're worth a fortune."

"You…you what? Sell people? Like slaves?" My hands shake and my knees turn so watery I can barely stand. "You're a trafficker?"

My body feels saturated by fear. My hand trembles as I run it along Ruby's side, feeling my way along. Her back bumper is gone. The dents in her body are fixed and sanded, leaving shiny spots of exposed metal.

"You'll get caught." No matter how sick his intentions are, I've got to keep talking. Keep minutes ticking off the clock in hopes Meg makes her call and the police are coming.

"People will look for me." I force the words out through gritted teeth. "If I don't show up at school, teachers and kids will ask what happened to me." Cold seeps through my feet from the smooth cement floor. It rises up my legs and through my body until my face and fingertips turn to ice.

"The cops. The FBI." I move around Ruby's back end. Her rear bumper is set off to the side, next to the front one. "Someone will call them."

"If someone was going to miss you that much," he says, tipping his head toward Ruby, "you wouldn't be living in your car." He shrugs his shoulders. "Street kids. The homeless. Drug addicts. They go missing all the time. No one pays attention."

I slide around Ruby until she's between me and the mechanic. "Where's our stuff? Did you toss it in the dumpster?" I inch along. "The cops will find it. Then they'll know for sure."

The mechanic steps around Ruby's back end. "Oh, you mean the stuffed animals and bags of little girl clothes?"

I stiffen. Meg. Of course he knows about Meg.

The mechanic nods toward the back door. "You weren't dumb enough to bring her, were you?"

My heart hammers in my chest.

His eyes narrow as he studies me. "She's outside? You brought her?" A flicker of excitement passes across his face, but the silence that follows terrifies me more than anything else he's said or done. It's a quiet, animal stillness, like the game's over and he's ready to pounce.

The tool bench is off to my side. Is that where he's pushing me? Trying to trap me there? Tools lay scattered along the top of the workbench and in piles along the floor. The right tool could be a weapon. Maybe the perfect weapon.

"You take advantage of people. Of their misfortune." I move closer to the bench, wary of being trapped between Ruby and the wall. My brain goes into hyperfocus, checking for tools, escape routes, hiding places.

"If I don't, someone else will." The mechanic's arms hang loosely at his sides, but his fingers twitch in a steady rhythm.

I reach for the workbench. My hand fumbles across the wooden surface until it closes over the metal handle of a wrench. I grab it and switch it to my other hand. "Money is more important than human lives?"

My fingers slide along the bench and bump into a piece of metal. I grab it—not sure what it is or how to use it—knowing I need every advantage I can find to fight.

The mechanic picks up his pace—not fast, just steady. I move quicker. He'll rush me, and I need to be ready, even though it's a cat-and-mouse power trip I'll never win.

I hold up my weapons while I back away. His quickened pace and the loose way he holds his hands out from his sides tells me he is done with my chatter. Done studying me. Done stalking me. I need a new plan.

My fingers wrap tighter around the metal in my hand. I take a quick breath, pull my arm back, and throw it straight at the light hanging over the workbench. The metal flies out of my hand, shattering the bulb and showering small slivers of glass over the tools.

Darkness hits me, but I'm already running. Two cars are parked near the front of the garage. I hold my hands out in front of me and hope I don't trip. My tennis shoes make slapping noises on the cement floor, giving away my direction. The wrench in my hand bashes against the car fender, sending echoes through the room.

Rapid footsteps thump across the cement after me. I run along the cold metal of the car as fast as I can, kicking off my tennis shoes as I go. When I get to the front fender, I angle toward the other car, running on tiptoes and sock feet. I hold my empty hand out in front of me and keep the metal wrench at my side.

I touch the car and slide along the driver's door and around the front bumper until I'm on the far side. I stop to listen. Nothing. In a space this big, there must be overhead lights, but the mechanic doesn't turn them on.

Sweat runs down my back and soaks my t-shirt. I concentrate, straining to hear the brush of a shoe or the bump of a body against metal. Nothing but my heart pounding in my ears. I crouch behind the car and focus on listening. Without struggling to see, my nerves calm and my heart rate slows.

Do I keep moving? I could smash right into him. Do I stay here and listen? Hope I hear him before he grabs me? I slowly straighten my legs and glance toward the back door and the window flanking it. The night makes dark gray squares in the flat black of the far wall. I could run for the door. Try to unlock it and be out of the garage before he gets to me. Then what? Grab Meg and run? If I got out the door, we wouldn't get ten feet before he'd catch me and Meg too. No. I trust in Meg and Jack and hope the police get here soon.

Metal crashes against metal. I jump and turn toward the far side of the room. Is he over there, or was that a diversion? I press against the side of the car and swing my gaze in a wide circle. One lighted dot near the front wall is the only break in the flat black ensnaring me. A light switch? A garage door opener?

Another crash, this time closer. A hand grabs my arm from the other side.

"Gotcha."

Muscles in my face and stomach contort, sending acid shooting up my throat. I yank myself away. The mechanic's grip crushes me until my wrench clatters to the floor. He pulls me tight against him, breathing into my hair. "I like playing games in the dark," he whispers.

Tears spill down my cheeks. "Monster!" His body molds itself against my back. I swing my free arm at his face, but he grabs my wrist and pushes me against the car. I squirm and twist, sickened by the closeness of his body.

The mechanic holds me so close I feel the stubble on his cheek against my face. "Your mom fought like this." His heart pounds against my back. "A real scrapper."

My body fills with such an ache, such a sadness for Mom, that my limbs turn weak and wobbly. The mechanic takes advantage, tightening his arms so much my upper body can't move. I try, but the more I wiggle, the harder he squeezes.

The mechanic is not a big man, but I feel small and frail wrapped in his hold. My head is forced against his shoulder and my back and bottom press against his body. His nearness makes my skin crawl and my stomach churn. I make myself relax, wait, breathe. All I need is one chance. Just one single instant and I'll be ready.

The mechanic locks us together so tight that his heart rate and breathing soon match my own. He waits. Seconds tick off the clock. I ache inside and out from the pressure. He slowly backs up, easing us away from the car. It's the moment I need.

I swing my feet up, plant them against the metal of the car, and shove as hard as I can. He doesn't expect the force, and the two of us topple over backward.

The mechanic hits the floor under me with a thud. Air flies out of his lungs in a whoosh and his arms loosen from the impact. I throw myself against his grip and roll away, scrambling to my feet and behind the car.

I need to hide, but where do I go that he won't find me? I close my eyes and listen. Soft brushing sounds float through the air. He grunts. I open my eyes, letting them sweep across the dark even though I can't see anything. It may be foolish not to keep moving, but I stay behind the car and listen for his breath.

I catch the sound of him stumbling against metal and freeze. The noise came from the far side, near Ruby and the workbench. I wait, my ears straining to pick up the tiniest of sounds. My heart pounds. My breaths are short. Shallow. Quiet.

I squat close to the floor and brush my fingers across the cement, light as a feather. I search for something to throw. Nothing. I balance and reach out farther. There. A screw? A bolt? Doesn't matter. It's small, but big enough for what I need. My fingers close around the scrap of metal and transfer it to my other hand. I feel for more, gathering a tiny arsenal.

Slowly, I stand, pick a piece of metal from my hand, and listen. No sounds. No hint of the mechanic. I throw the metal to the front near the door. *Back at you*, I whisper in the silence of my head.

The noise is only a ping. It is a small sound, but big enough to cause the mechanic to make the tiniest of mistakes. A stumble? A quick movement against a car? Enough for me to hear him.

I can't stand still and throw screws and bolts across the room. The mechanic is smart enough to look in the one place with no noise. I ease away from the car and inch toward the tiny dot of light shining in the front corner.

My feet—soft and light—touch the cement, feeling for a clear path. Breath enters my lungs in shallow whiffs. No noise leaves my lips. My heart slows to match.

Halfway across the front of the garage, I throw another bit of metal. The tiny ping bounces off the opposite wall. I wait, but I don't hear a scrape, stumble, or sound.

I inch toward the tiny dot of light until I can press tight against the wall. The last place I should be is backed into a corner, but hopefully it's also the last place the mechanic will look.

I wait, pushed into the corner, silent and alone. My knees shake, and my legs grow weak from fear and fatigue. I stiffen them, letting the minutes slide by, each one filling me with hope and energy that I'll survive. Meg will make the call. She will. I know she will.

"Game over." His voice is so close that it shocks me with his nearness.

I strike with my fist, but he's got my arm before I can connect. I swing the other one, but he gets that one too and twists them both so hard my bones threaten to snap.

The mechanic leans toward me, the smell of his breath robbing me of air. "Guys pay fortunes for this kind of fun."

I kick out with my foot and connect with his shin. He grunts, but doesn't loosen his grip. "You soulless creep!" I spit the words into his face. "You empty…heartless…" But words can't describe such sickness. Such evil.

The mechanic is so close we're cheek to cheek, pressed together like lovers. "It's not about you, honey," he whispers in my ear. "It's business. Remember?"

I twist and turn to fight, but he's stronger. Bigger. He picks me up, dragging me out of my corner refuge. My feet flail against his shins, but he doesn't care.

CHAPTER TWENTY-FOUR

THE BACK DOOR CRASHES BACK on its hinges. "Police!"

His grip loosens enough for me to pull my arm free. I slam my hand at the button by the garage door. "Help! Please help!"

The door rumbles to life, inching its way off the floor. The mechanic spins me around and wraps his arm across my chest, locking me in front of his body. I fight until cold metal presses against the softness of my cheek. I don't have to see the gun to recognize the icy hardness and rounded barrel. Was it tucked in the waistband of his jeans all this time? Or did he pick it up when I was hiding?

"Police! Put your hands on your head! Walk out, slow and steady!"

"Help! He's got a—" The mechanic shifts the gun away from my cheek and clamps his other hand across my mouth. He squeezes so tight against my nose I can hardly breathe. I struggle against him, but his thumb pushes down, cutting off my air. The garage door slowly rumbles open, and all I can think about is breathing. I can't fight his grip without air. I ache for one good breath, but all I get are tiny whiffs through my smashed lips and pinched nose.

The mechanic shoves me forward. "Shoot and she's dead." He yells the words right next to my ear. I stumble, my stocking feet trampling against his. He pulls my head back and up. His other arm pins me, the gun now pressing hard against my side. I can't see anything but the black ceiling of the garage. He thrusts me forward until we're under the dark gray of night.

"Drop the girl!"

Tears leak out of the corners of my eyes. Meg. Meg called the police. She's safe, and even if I die right here in a blaze of bullets, someone will take care of her. And Mom—if she's still alive, the police will find her.

The mechanic pulls me along. "Back away, all of you." He states his orders in the same calm manner he described trafficking human lives. "One mistake and she's dead."

"And then you're wanted for murder," says a cop.

The mechanic tightens his grip on my mouth and shrugs his head to the right. "Over there. Guys behind the garage too."

He's still. Relaxed. His body is tight against mine, but there is no tension. No fear oozing through his skin. We wait. Boots scrape on pavement. Bodies shuffle away from us. Equipment creaks and groans, but the police are silent. I feel their movement, but can't see any of it. I study the roof. The sky. Search for stars, knowing it's too early to catch their bright twinkles of light.

"Turn your backs." The mechanic's breath brushes across the side of my face, but I'm numb to his nearness.

More shuffles and scrapes, creaks and groans.

"Face down on the pavement."

"No way," yells one of the cops.

"Down or she's dead." The mechanic doesn't yell, just insists in that calm, vile tone. My life rests in the hands of this heartless man. One wrong turn—or a trigger-happy cop—and I am dead.

My head aches as I struggle to breathe. I listen to the last of the sounds before the night turns silent. No clank of equipment. No boots on pavement. Nothing but a deep, eerie stillness.

The mechanic backs away, dragging me with him. Slow. Steady. I should struggle, should fight him, but all my energy goes into pulling tiny wisps of air into my aching lungs.

The pavement changes to sidewalk under my toes. "No one moves or the girl dies," he says again. This time, the words startle me, shocking me out of the fog that seeps through my aching head. Will he kill me anyway, even if the police do everything he asks?

The mechanic pulls me backward, farther and farther away from the garage. I concentrate on the cement under my stocking feet, feeling for every break in the concrete. Rooftops slide by, but my vision blurs. I struggle to stay alert.

The mechanic drops his hand from my nose and mouth. Surprised, I try to breathe, but my lungs don't respond. Too late, I remember to struggle and yell, but my movements and voice are sluggish and slow. He shifts the arm across my chest. It's the one with the gun. Do I fight or freeze? I take my chances and thrust my weight against his arm.

The mechanic throws me to the pavement, and my head hits with a crack. Bright flashes of light dance in front of my eyes. I can't feel or see what is happening. All I can do is lay on my back, staring at the stars swirling in front of me. All I can do is suck air into my starving lungs.

I am alive. I am breathing.

CHAPTER TWENTY-FIVE

MOM. I`VE GOT TO GET TO MOM. Tell her to hang on. Make sure she's alive. I roll to my side and try to push myself to my hands and knees, but my head is throbbing.

Gunshots crack and pop. Voices call orders over my head. Boots pound past me. Officer Rodriguez hovers by my face. "You crazy girl. Why did you do this by yourself? Why didn't you call me last night?"

My voice doesn't work. My throat is so dry it takes all my effort to speak. "You made it," I whisper.

"I got your message. We were already on the way when your sister called."

"Meg?" The word is barely louder than my breath.

"In my car with your boyfriend. Worried as hell, but okay."

I try to stand, but my head pounds. Officer Rodriguez presses me back against the pavement until I am flat on my back. "Stay down."

"The mechanic?"

"We'll find him." Officer Rodriguez squeezes my shoulder.

"Mom." I reach for his arm. "Get Mom." My voice wobbles and my vision swims. "She's in that room. That room over the office."

His hand stays firm against my shoulder. "We're on it, Mattie. Just stay down."

"Go now." Tears leak down my cheeks. "Please?" I grip the fabric of his shirtsleeve. "Please?"

"Stay flat. Promise?"

His request feels cruel, like acid burning my throat. I ache to run back to the garage, fly up the stairs, and wrap my arms around Mom. I need to know she's like me: scared, traumatized, but alive. I loosen my grip and let that be my answer.

Officer Rodriguez keeps pressure on my shoulder and waves over another officer. I try to follow everything that's happening, but my eyelids slowly slide shut. I work at prying them open, but give up and listen to the activity surging over me. Rodriguez's heavy hand leaves and a lighter one takes its place.

Is it relief that's making me so weak and drowsy? Meg is safe with Jack in the back of a squad car and the police will get Mom.

"Blink if you can hear me."

My eyes fly open. The face of a young woman hovers over me. Was I sleeping? How long? Where is Mom? Where is Meg?

A light shines in my eyes. "Hmmm," she says.

I stare into the glare. "Mom?"

"We're getting her," the woman says. "I need you to follow the light, okay?"

"I need to get up," I whisper. "To see her. Please?"

"Not yet, honey. You've had a bad crack on the head."

A male EMT wraps a collar around my neck and puts plastic tubing under my nose. A cool stream of oxygen flows into my lungs. They lift me onto a flat board, strapping down my body and head. The EMTs raise me to a gurney and cover me with a warm blanket. Only then do I tremble from the cold.

Their speed and efficiency confuses me. The gurney starts to move, and I panic. Will they let me see Meg and Mom before whisking me off to a hospital?

"Meg?" My voice barely reaches the EMT at the head of my gurney. "Mom?"

"Mattie!"

I can't move my head to see her, but the pounding of her tennis shoes tells me she is running. "Meg?" The gurney wobbles and my sister is beside me.

"I was so scared," she cries. "So scared."

"Me too." My words catch in my throat, fighting for space with sobs of relief. "Me too."

My gurney wobbles again as Meg climbs up its side.

"Hey," the EMT reaches for Meg. "Get down, kid. You can't be up there."

Meg kicks at the guy. "I'm not getting down, and you can't make me!" She scrambles the last few inches and throws herself beside me.

"Mattie!" Jack appears beside my bed. "Are you okay?"

My eyes and lower arms are the only parts of my body I can move. I grip my sister's hand. "Thanks, Jack. Thanks for taking care of Meg."

"My God, Mattie," he says. "I...I'll do anything. Anything you need. Just...just let me know."

I turn my eyes back to the EMTs and look from one to the other. "Don't separate Meg and me. Do you hear me? Don't separate us." My voice sounds raspy and low, not at all normal. "We're not leaving until we see Mom."

The woman leans over me. "We've got to take you in, Mattie." She gives me a sad smile. "It's cold out here, and you've got a bad concussion."

"I'll scream. Fight." I force my voice to be strong.

Meg twists around and yells, "And I'll kick and bite and punch and you will be really, really sorry you didn't let us see Mommy."

I am tired and weak, but I piece together every bit of strength I have to prepare myself for battle. The EMTs back away, and Meg snuggles next to me. My body is rigid. Tense from worry. Are they getting a needle full of drugs ready to shoot into my arm? Will I be asleep in minutes? Meg could be put in foster care without me there to protect her.

The EMT returns, but he has a sideways grin and an arm full of blankets. "You win, girls." He spreads warm layers over us and tucks them in tight. "You've been through enough without fighting us too." He tops off our mound of covers with a foil blanket.

Tears slide down my cheeks and soak into the padding around my head. "Thanks. Thanks a lot." The EMTs stay close, but they let us lie in our cocoon—warm and safe and together.

Jack's fingers brush across my cheek. "I'm right here, Mattie. Right beside you if you need me."

"I owe you, Jack." I press my lips together to keep from breaking into sobs.

Meg tightens her grip on me and whispers, "You'll be okay, Mattie, and so will Mommy." Her little hand pats my shoulder. "We'll get a house and we'll start over. Just the three of us. And we'll be so happy because we will be together and never be apart again. Forever and ever and ever."

Meg's words comfort me, like she's the sixteen-year-old and I'm six. They are a little girl's words, but her thoughts are my thoughts and my dreams. And even if Meg and I end up in foster care, I'll fight to keep us together so that I never have to leave her alone again.

Activity swirls around us. Cops come and go. EMTs rush past carrying equipment. I grip Meg's hand so tight I'm afraid of hurting her.

Finding Mom wasn't supposed to be like this. When I thought she was in Darren's apartment, I pictured her bound and gagged like in one of those old black-and-white movies. Alert. Whole. Relieved to see us and scared, but not really harmed. I'd untie Mom and we'd hug and cry and carry on about how scared we were. Meg and Mom and I would be together, distressed by what we'd been through, but whole and happy.

How could I have been such a child? So naive. So full of storybook endings that I shut out the ugly truth of the real world. The mechanic was cold and inhuman enough to sell people to the highest bidder. How can a person lack those basic bits of compassion that even animals feel for each other?

Meg squirms around until she can look me in the face. "Why don't the police people and the ambulance people bring Mommy? Why are they so slow?"

Her face wrinkles with worry, making me want to paint over the ugly truth of Mom's ordeal. But Meg isn't that same baby girl she was a week ago. "She's hurt, Meg." I swallow the lump rising in my throat. "Probably pretty bad."

Tears turn Meg's eyes into watery pools. "But we've got each other," I say, "and if Mom comes back, we'll help her get better. Okay?"

Meg's lips quiver, and she lies next to me, her small body shaking. I hold her hand and whisper words like "It's okay" and "We're together" over and over.

I breathe in the warmth of my little sister and replay memories of Mom in my head. Like how she smiles when she sees us come in the door and laughs at Meg's knock-knock jokes, even when they don't make any sense. How she keeps the apartment clean, cooks our meals, and scrubs our clothes. How she loves us no matter how snotty we get.

Mom's life would've been so much easier if she'd given me away when I was born. Instead, she raised me with love and kindness. Something the mechanic knows nothing about.

Officer Rodriguez walks to our gurney. His face softens, and a hint of a smile flips up one side of his mouth. Meg pops up, ripping open our cozy little cocoon. My heart soars.

"She's alive." He glances between Meg and me. "She's pretty beat up and not totally conscious, but she's one tough lady. Just like her daughters."

So many tears stream down my face that I can barely see through them. Meg claps her hands and squeals.

Jack's hand squeezes my shoulder. "That's great, Mattie."

"We want to see her," I say. "We have to."

"It'd be better if you waited." His brown eyes zero in on me. They are soft and kind, but they tell me that Mom is hurt more than he wants to say.

"We have to see her," I repeat.

Officer Rodriguez studies me before turning to Meg. "You stay here until we bring your mom over, got it?"

Meg bounces, rocking my gurney with her excitement. "Got it."

Officer Rodriguez moves away, and the garage grows quiet and still. The EMTs beside me turn to watch. I can't see what is happening, so I picture Mom being brought from that ugly prison of a room. I see her lying on a board like mine, suffering and in pain, but living and breathing, with her heart pumping strong and true. I listen to directions bouncing back and forth between the EMTs.

"Easy now."

"I got her."

"Slow and steady."

"Tell me what's happening, Meg." I squeeze her hand. "I can't see, so tell me everything."

"Mommy's all strapped down like you, with one ambulance guy on each end of the board. It's really narrow stairs so they've got to be really, really careful." Meg stops to take a breath. "And now they are putting her on a wheely bed like yours and tying her down like you, and—"

Meg scrambles from my bed and is gone.

"Meg?" I stare at the darkness over my head, feeling more lost and alone than ever. I can't see Mom or hold her, brush her long hair away from her face. I can't do any of the sweet, comforting things she always does for me.

Sobs surge through my body. I fight the straps holding me. "Mom!" I scream. "Mom!"

Jack's hand grips my shoulder and his face hovers over me. "Hold still, Mattie. She's coming."

I force myself to relax. To breathe. I listen to the brush of feet on concrete and the soft turning of wheels. I feel the movement of people. Excitement surges through me. "Mom?"

Meg grabs my hand. "Mommy's right here. Right beside us."

CHAPTER TWENTY-SIX

COLUMBIA HIGH SCHOOL LOOKS WORN OUT. Overused. In the weeks I've been gone, it's as if the bricks and cream-colored paint have a ton more chips and the gray cement sidewalk picked up dozens more dings. The whole place looks tired, like it's way older than its years. Or maybe that's me projecting my life on the walls, windows, and doors of the place.

Mom drives toward the lot near the front door. Ruby's window and taillights are fixed, and Officer Rodriguez put her bumpers back on for free. In the damp Oregon weather, Ruby's spots of exposed metal would rust, so Mom bought some cheap red paint at an auto store and sprayed them. Now Ruby's got splotches of red that don't quite match the rest of her body—scars she'll carry for the rest of her life, like Mom and Meg and me.

Our family's scars aren't as visible as Ruby's. No one can see that our innocence is gone. People can't look at us and know we carry a distrust in humanity so deep it breaks our confidence.

We have other scars too. Bad dreams. Anxiety. Worries that we'll be torn apart and separated forever. Time will help, but no amount of time will erase the fear of being homeless and vulnerable.

Mom's story came out in pieces. Maybe she thought she was protecting us, or maybe she couldn't face telling us the whole ugly tale.

The mechanic offered to pick up Ruby at 7-Eleven and deliver her back at the end of the day. It was a perfect solution, but when he brought Ruby back with the window and taillights fixed, he asked Mom to drop him off. She should have texted me, but she was in a hurry and almost out of cell time, so she got into the car.

Mom fought, but like me, was no match for his strength. She made mistakes, a ton of them, but I understand why—she was hungry, exhausted, and living in a state of constant stress. The abuse of Mom's body is healing, but her internal scars will be harder to survive.

The mechanic is in jail, caught that same night by a squad car down the street from the garage. Knowing he is locked away should relieve us, but his arrest brings its own set of worries. At his trial, Mom and I have to sit on the witness stand, look into his eyes, and relive every ugly detail of our capture. We have to admit to our vulnerability and mistakes and hope a jury puts him in jail.

Mom parks Ruby in a visitor's space near the front door. I watch the rain sliding down the windshield in wiggly little rivers, but I'm not ready to get out of the car. Driving up to

Columbia reminds me that I am a different person than the one who went to school here.

I turn to Mom and suck in a long, slow breath, pulling air deep into my body. "I might be a while."

Mom nods. The sorrow in her eyes clashes with the soft beauty of her face. "Take your time, baby. Meg and I will be fine."

I reach across the car and squeeze Mom's knee, my eyes never leaving her face. She gives me a tight little smile and lays her one good hand over mine. Her other pokes out of a sling, holding her broken arm against her chest. "Go." She nods her head toward the school.

I step out of the car and stand in the rain. Water drips onto my head, sliding in cold streams down my face. Today is our first day back as a family. The first day we can move forward into a life together, inch by tiny inch.

Again I was naive, thinking that once I found Mom, the three of us would be back together. That didn't happen. Mom left the garage in one ambulance, and Meg and I went in another. A caseworker stayed overnight with us at the hospital, but we didn't get to see Mom.

The next day, Meg and I were taken to a foster home where we lived with an old man and woman who fed us, gave us a place to sleep, and included us in their Thanksgiving and Christmas celebrations. They lived too far from our schools, so we worked on homework sent to us over the internet.

The old people were kind and caring, but Mom wasn't allowed to come to their house. After she got out of the hospital, she lived at the Mission in the women's dorm. We only saw her four times in all those weeks.

Meg and I would probably still be in that foster home, separated by red tape and good intentions, if Officer Rodriguez hadn't found us a room in a home for women and children. We can only stay for six months, but that will give Mom time to save money for an apartment.

I walk through the parking lot and go inside. Before I clean out my locker, I stop at the office to do paperwork. No one hugs me and says they'll miss me like the office workers did for Meg at her school. This is high school. Kids come and go; people care, but there are too many of us to keep track of. By the time I finish the transfer papers, it's first lunch and the halls are busy with kids.

I head toward my locker. My week with Jack seems like a lifetime ago. Like I was a different person when I knew him; like he was just a make-believe boyfriend and not real-life flesh and bone. Maybe he was. Maybe I'll get my stuff from my locker, head right back to Ruby, and let our romance stay that way—a beautiful story, a fairy tale that kept me trudging on when life got too tough to handle.

Jack rescued Meg from the alley that night. I am forever grateful to him for that, but the first days Meg and I were in foster care, he texted and called me all the time. He didn't understand why we couldn't live at his house or why there were no apartments that people like us could afford. Jack offered us money from his parents and begged me to take it. I wouldn't. In some ways, these last weeks were more confusing for Jack than me.

Asking him to stop calling and texting felt mean and unfair, but I needed time to sleep, eat enough food to feel normal, and curl up in front of TV reruns without pressure from anyone. Meg and I needed to read every children's book in the foster home, be safe in our own little bubble, and let the outside world move on without us.

I head down junior hall, turn into my locker bay, and stop with a jolt. A girl behind me growls about paying attention, but all I can do is stare. My locker is covered in sticky notes. Pink. Yellow. Neon green. A rainbow of messages stuck all over the door.

I walk forward and read *Miss you* and *Miss you more* and *Really, really, missing you now*. Over and over again, I read words telling me how much Jack cared, how much he wanted to share lunch, a quick conversation, or a lingering look. How much he wanted me to be safe.

I spin the dial on my lock, open the door, and pull out all my stuff. I pack my backpack full of papers, pencils, and half-filled notebooks. My textbooks get stacked on the floor until I get the last of my junk cleaned out. I slam the door and spend a long time staring at Jack's sweet little notes before peeling each one off the metal, stacking them together, and tucking them into the front pocket of my pack. I pick up the stack of textbooks and head to the library to drop them off.

When I leave the library, I turn and head straight for the front door. Walking away is best for both of us. I just go. Clean and quick. Jack lives in a different world and has opportunities that I will never experience. Even if I qualify for a college scholarship, I'll have to work long hours and save every bit of money I can for Mom, Meg, and me to be financially safe.

Once I'm out of his world, Jack can go off to college, play basketball, and meet girls that aren't struggling to survive. And me? I will have beautiful memories and a stack of sticky notes to tell me that in my junior year of high school, one really nice guy cared about me.

I'm all the way back to the office before I slow to a stop. I may be poor, and I may be homeless, but one thing I'm not is a coward. I lived in a car, slept in a dumpster, and fought off a man with so little soul he could sell people into a life of horror. But now, when it comes to someone I really care about—someone who came to my rescue when I needed him—I choose to be wimpy and weak instead of brave, or at least kind. I'm slinking out of Jack's life without even offering him a decent goodbye.

I turn and stare down the hall toward the cafeteria. Old fears assault me. I could walk back and see if he's sitting at our table. But what if he's hanging out with a bunch of his friends? Laughing. Talking. Horsing around. I can't walk up to him in a crowd like that.

More fears hit me. Am I strong enough to handle Jack's friendship, maybe even his love, without giving up on college, law school, and being President? And what about Jack? Can he handle the world I live in?

There are too many questions, too many unknowns in our relationship, but one thing I feel in the pit of my stomach is that Jack deserves a chance. He cares about me and Meg too. Everything he's ever done, from the Saturday he bought us McDonald's to the sticky notes he left on my locker, confirms that much. Not knowing what happened to us must be tearing him up.

I pull out my phone and type out a text. *Hey. Want to meet for coffee at the downtown library? Sunday @ 2?*

I slide my phone into my pocket and walk out of the school. Meg sits in the back seat of Ruby and gives me a grin and that crazy two-handed wave of hers. Mom is watching for me too. Her good hand raises just enough. She doesn't want to embarrass me, but she can't help letting me know how much she loves me.

My phone dings in my pocket. I pull it out while I walk to the car and smile at Jack's text. *Yes!!!!* ☹ ← *Me before your text.* ☺ ☺ ☺ ← *Me after your text.*

I type *See you Sunday* and climb into Ruby.

Mom drives us across Eugene, over the I-5 freeway to Springfield and our new home. It is a plain two-story box of a house with a black, pitched roof, tan siding, and white trim. It's no bigger than the others on the street, but to my little family, it's a palace of the grandest proportions. We walk up to the front door, and Mom reaches out to press the doorbell. The roof of the small front porch keeps off the drizzle of a cold winter rain.

A woman in tight jeans and a crisp white shirt answers the door. "Rita Rollins?" The woman extends her arm to usher us in. "Come in. Come in." She is a lot taller than Mom, but not much older.

We step inside. The front door leads to a large living room that is furnished in well-worn hand-me-downs. The tan couch sags, and the two green chairs don't match each other or anything else in the room. One lampshade sits at an odd angle; the other one has a small rip in the side. The end tables are stained and chipped, but it is the most beautiful living room I have ever seen.

The woman holds out her hand. "I'm Allie, the resident assistant here." Mom shakes her hand and introduces us to this stranger who will share our lives for the next few months.

Allie throws her arm toward the back of the house. "Let me show you around."

We follow Allie through a kitchen, where she explains how the residents take turns cooking communal dinners and cleaning up afterwards. She points to a small cupboard we can use for our own food. Meg giggles, puts her hand to the side of her mouth, and whispers, "For our bread and peanut butter."

Upstairs, Allie shows us to the bathroom we will share, with its tub, shower, and toilet. The entire house has a lived-in quality, but at the same time it is spotlessly clean. Last—and best of all—she finishes our tour at a bedroom near the end of the hall.

Allie hands a set of keys to Mom. "The big one is for the front and back door, and the smaller one is for this room." She smiles. "Move in and get settled. If you have any questions, my room is off the downstairs hall, first door on the right."

Mom unlocks the door. We step into our room and look around in wonder, running our hands over the blue flowered quilts on the bunk beds and along the scratched tops of two mismatched dressers. We gaze out the window at bare limbs on a big maple tree and open the little closet that waits for the few clothes, toys, and shoes that we own.

"It's beautiful," whispers Mom. "Just beautiful."

Meg twirls around in a circle. "And after we get my dollhouse and Mattie's books from Darren, it will look just like home."

Mom and I lean into a hug and gather Meg in with us. Tears run down my face, but this time they are not from fear or worry. This time, my tears are pure joy.

AUTHOR`S NOTE

SLEEPING IN MY JEANS IS a work of fiction, yet the story of Rita, Mattie, and Meg is all too real. State statistics for the 2016–2017 school year tell us that 22,541 students in Oregon did not have a safe place to call home. Not all of these students are on the street or in a car like Mattie and her family, but even though they may have a roof over their heads, they live in a state of constant turmoil.

Another social issue that appears in this novel is human trafficking. I-5 is known as the West Coast Track and considered a major network for sex trafficking from Canada to Mexico. It is a serious problem that needs attention and legislation.

Resources:
    "Record Number of Homeless Students" by Molly Harbarger
        for the *Oregonian/Oregon Live*, November 17, 2017
    "Oregon's Homeless Student Population Rises Third
        Year in a Row" by Chris Lehman for Oregon Public
        Broadcasting (OPB), November 22, 2016
    "On Track: Sexual Exploitation Along the I-5 Corridor"
        by Dylan Wells for *The Gate*, January 9, 2017

A portion of the sales of *Sleeping in My Jeans* will be donated to:
    St. Vincent de Paul Society of Lane County (*Youth House
        for homeless teen girls and other affordable housing
        projects*)
    www.svdp.us
    P.O. Box 24608
    Eugene, Oregon 97402

ACKNOWLEDGMENTS

MANY THANKS TO MACKENZIE DEATER and Monique Vieu, my project managers at Ooligan. Your hard work, expertise, and dedication to detail are much admired and greatly appreciated. And to Lisa Hein, my editing manager. You took *Sleeping* from a good story in a rough package to a place of beauty.

Thanks to Ooligan Press for believing in *Sleeping* and doing the hard work to make it happen, starting with Maeko Bradshaw, Vi La Bianca, Alison Cantrell, and the amazing team listed on the last page. I am forever grateful for your time, energy, and talent.

Thanks to Karen Myers, John Reed, and Terri Gassman for your excellent advice, and John and Maria Rudy for that last edit.

Thanks to the Eugene Police Department and the Eugene City Library for answering so many questions.

Thanks to family and friends for believing in me, encouraging me to keep writing, and for reading all those early drafts.

A special thanks to Kristen, Robby, Ben, Matt, Kevin, Rhiannon, Jess, Colin, Carter, Cadence, Carys, Julian, and Caleb. Family is the central theme of this novel, and you continue to prove it is the core of my life.

And most of all, thanks to Bob, for loving me.

ABOUT THE AUTHOR

CONNIE KING LEONARD IS A WRITER of books for children and teens. She holds degrees in education from Minot State University and the University of Oregon, and she has taught both elementary and middle school. Her years teaching provided the inspiration for this novel; in 2017, an estimated 22,541 students in the Oregon school system found themselves houseless for some part of the year, and every year the number is rising. *Sleeping in My Jeans* works to give these children a voice and a story. Connie is a member of SCBWI as well as Willamette Writers, and in 2008, she won the Kay Snow award for children's writing with *Too Much Glue, Gertie*. Connie lives in Milwaukie, Oregon, with her husband Bob.

OOLIGAN PRESS

OOLIGAN PRESS IS A STUDENT-RUN publishing house rooted in the rich literary culture of the Pacific Northwest. Founded in 2001 as part of Portland State University's Department of English, Ooligan is dedicated to the art and craft of publishing. Students pursuing master's degrees in book publishing staff the press in an apprenticeship program under the guidance of a core faculty of publishing professionals.

Project Managers
Mackenzie Deater
Monique Vieu

Project Team
Stephanie Anderson
Terence Brierly
Jessica DeBolt
Grace Evans
Katie Fairchild
Jasmine Gower
Des Hewson
Kelly Hogan
Stephen Hyde
Hilary Louth
Kristen Ludwigsen
Scott MacDonald
Laura Nutter
Riley Pittenger
Victoria Reilly
Maki Takase
Lynette Wolf
Michelle Zhang

Acquisitions
Maeko Bradshaw
Vi La Bianca
Alison Cantrell
Alyssa Schaffer
Desiree Wilson

Editorial
Lisa Hein
Hilary Louth
Stephanie Anderson
Mackenzie Deater
Jessica DeBolt
Alison Cantrell
Katie Fairchild
Brittney Finato
Michele Ford
Jasmine Gower
Elise Hitchings
Kelly Hogan
Kristen Ludwigsen
Karissa Mathae
Amylia Ryan

Thomas Spölhof
Joanna Szabo
Monique Vieu

Design
Andrea McDonald
Jenny Kimura
Bridget Carrick

Digital
Stephanie Argy
Kaitlin Barnes

Marketing
Morgan Nicholson
Sydney Kiest

Social Media
Katie Fairchild
Sadie Moses